ALSO BY JOHN WILSON

YOUNG ADULT FICTION

Shot at Dawn

Written in Blood

Ghost Moon

Victorio's War

Death on the River

Red Goodwin

Adrift in Time

Ghosts of James Bay

Across Frozen Seas

Flames of the Tiger

And in the Morning

Flags of War

Broken Arrow

Wings of War (Book One in the Tales of War series)

YOUNG ADULT NON-FICTION

Desperate Glory: The Story of WWI

Failed Hope: The Story of the Lost Peace

Bitter Ashes: The Story of WWII

Righting Wrongs: The Story of Norman Bethune

Discovering the Arctic: The Story of John Rae

Norman Bethune: A Life of Passionate Conviction

John Franklin: Traveller on Undiscovered Seas

AVAILABLE ONLY AS EBOOKS

The Alchemist's Dream

The Final Alchemy

The Heretic's Secret

Where Soldiers Lie

Germania

Four Steps to Death

Lost in Spain

The Weet Trilogy

Battle Scars

North with Franklin: The Lost Journals of James Fitzjames

Ghost Mountains and Vanished Oceans: North America from Birth to Middle-Age.

DARK TERROR

JOHN WILSON

DOUBLEDAY CANADA

Doubleday Canada and colophon are registered trademarks
of Random House of Canada Limited

Library and Archives Canada Cataloguing in Publication

Wilson, John (John Alexander), 1951-, author
Dark terror / John Wilson.

Issued in print and electronic formats.
ISBN 978-0-385-67832-2 (pbk.).—ISBN 978-0-385-67833-9 (epub)

I. Title.

PS8595.I5834D37 2015   jC813'.54   C2015-901940-0
                                              C2015-901941-9

Cover image: barbed wire © Lochstampfer/Dreamstime.com;
pick-ax © Twilightartpictures/Dreamstime.com
Cover design: Rachel Cooper

Printed and bound in the USA

Published in Canada by Doubleday Canada,
a division of Random House of Canada Limited,
a Penguin Random House Company

www.penguinrandomhouse.ca

10 9 8 7 6 5 4 3 2 1

Penguin
Random House
DOUBLEDAY CANADA

*Dedicated to the tunnelers of all sides who lived,
fought and died in the darkness beneath the trenches.*

CHAPTER 1

Cave-in—June 7, 1915

I will die, trapped like my uncle Frank, lungs straining painfully to fill in an airless black hole beneath thousands of tons of rock. Alec Shorecross will be one more sad name carved on a miners' memorial. That was my first thought when I heard the deep, grumbling bump in the rock and felt the pressure wave pass through the air. I've been underground long enough to know what that bump means. Somewhere, back along the narrow tunnel that is my only way out, the pressure in the rock has become too much and the roof has collapsed or a sidewall has blown in.

When I calm down, I begin to think more rationally. With luck, it won't be a complete blockage and I'll be able to squeeze back through. If not, I'll have to rely on the mine crew on the other side of the fall digging me out. I should be all right. There's plenty of air in this tunnel to last me a long time. Water might be more of a problem, but I've seen moisture running down the walls, so I can soak up some with my handkerchief to keep me going. I'll get hungry, but I can last a long time without food. My situation's nothing like Uncle Frank's. He was in a tiny space with five other men, surrounded by hundreds of tons of rock. It took the mine crew almost two weeks to dig through to them, and by then they were all long dead from suffocation. One man had managed to scratch the words "Good-bye, my love" on the tunnel wall above their huddled bodies.

My carbide lamp is throwing a comforting warm light ahead of me as I work my way back along the old drift toward the fall. My great fear is having a leg or an arm crushed by a falling rock or a foot taken off by a runaway ore trolley. Every day I see what that did to my dad after his leg was destroyed by a fall. I see how he sits at home, glowering into the fire, silently bitter at being unable to work and wracked with guilt that he can't support his family anymore. That's why I came to work in the Terra Nova copper mine as soon as I could—to be the breadwinner for the family, to try to ease my mother's careworn face. That was 1910, when I'd just turned ten and was only allowed to be an ore picker on the surface. Now it's the summer of 1915 and I've been underground for two years. Way things are going, I'll be out of work long before I turn sixteen.

The mine's scheduled to close in a month or two, and I'm in this tunnel now because the shift boss sent me and Jack Foster to search this old worked-out area for signs of any copper ore that had been missed. Anything we find might keep the mine open longer— and keep us earning thirteen cents an hour for a few weeks more—so we're happy to do it. Thing is, Jack's not here. I'm on my own.

Jack grew up on a farm down south and moved here when his dad came up to look after the pit ponies. My friend spends more of his spare time with the ponies than he does with the other miners. "Poor beasts," he's always saying. "Having to spend their whole lives underground and never seeing a sunrise." I point out that almost eternal darkness is a human miner's lot as well, but Jack won't listen.

Last night, Jack's favorite pony, a sturdy little beast called Samson, was taken sick with colic, and Jack was desperate to check on him before we set off. I told him to go on. I said I'd head down the drift and he could catch up once he'd comforted his friend. It was dumb to come here alone, but at least Jack knows where I am.

A PIT PONY UNDERGROUND.

He's probably already organizing men to come and dig me out.

I turn a corner and stare into the bright cone cast by my lamp—the drift is completely blocked. I step forward and my light dances over the rock as I examine the wall that lies between me and freedom. There are a few blocks small enough that I could move them out of the way, but there's no point. Most are so big and so firmly wedged in place that I would simply exhaust myself trying. My only hope is that Jack and the others can dig through to me from the far side before I die of thirst, hunger or suffocation.

I put my ear against a large rock and listen for the

noise of digging—nothing, but it's early yet. The men will have heard or felt the bump. They may even have found the fall, but it will take time to bring down equipment so that they can begin work. I move back around the corner—away from the fall—in case loose pieces of rock are ready to come down. I sit down against the tunnel wall and switch off my carbide lamp to conserve fuel. The darkness envelops me like a thick blanket. Normally darkness doesn't bother me, but I can't help thinking that this is the darkness of death.

I begin to imagine all sorts of horrors. What if the fall is too wide to get through, or the roof too unstable to allow heavy work? What if Jack was already on his way to meet me and is dead under the fall? If that's the case, we might not even be missed until shift's end. My throat feels dry and constricted; my stomach is cramping and my breath coming in short, shallow gasps. I'm dying.

I clench my right fist, lift it to my mouth and bite down hard on the knuckles until I notice the salty taste of blood. The pain cuts through my panic attack. I'm being stupid. It's only been minutes since the fall. I can't possibly be dying already. I force myself to breathe slowly and regularly: in through my nose, out through my mouth. I suck my teeth to produce saliva, swirl it round my mouth and swallow. My stomach settles, my chest relaxes and my heart rate slows. I must have patience, but waiting is difficult. Time passes at a different speed in the lonely darkness. With no watch, a minute can seem like an hour; with no sun or moon, an hour can seem like a day.

I take a deep breath and try to think about what I will do when I get out. Jack's a couple of years older than me and says he's going to join the army. "Nothing else for us here," he says. I point out that things are bound to improve, that if the war goes on, there's going to be a big demand for copper and iron ore. But Jack scoffs at that. "So we have the choice of mining or fishing. Not even enough soil up here to farm anything." He keeps showing me posters asking for volunteers to swell the ranks of the Newfoundland Regiment, and newspaper cuttings saying what a wonderful time the first volunteers are having training in England. His latest pitch is the news that the regiment is headed for Egypt. "Imagine that! Egypt! You can't deny that Egypt's more exotic than Coachman's Cove: sunshine, pyramids and girls as beautiful as Cleopatra. And you get free rations and a dollar a day."

I have to admit that the Newfoundlanders do seem to be having a good time and seeing Egypt *would* be something, but war's not all fun and games. Sooner or later the regiment's going to have to do its bit in the fighting. Not that I'm afraid of doing my bit—I suppose I'll have to if the war doesn't stop soon—but despite the cheerful battle reports in the newspapers, it's obvious things are not going well. Back in March, the newspapers trumpeted the Battle of Neuve Chapelle as a famous victory, but the twelve thousand killed and wounded seems a very high price to pay for what little was gained. This war is not like the wars of old. There are no Waterloos that decide something in one day. I think the chances of dying in this war might be very high.

I laugh out loud. Here I am thinking about the chances of being killed in a war I haven't even joined yet, and I'm in much greater danger here, trapped in a hole in the ground. Maybe, after they dig me out, I will go with Jack and join up. I look older than my years, and from what I hear, the recruiters aren't being too choosy. At least in the army I'll get to see some of the world outside northern Newfoundland.

I must have drifted off to sleep, because I wake up to a terrifying crash. My first thought is that it's another cave-in, but then I hear Jack's voice calling my name. I stumble back around the corner of the drift to see my friend's cheerful face sticking through a hole in the fall. He's holding a carbide lamp in his right hand and waving it about, making shadows swim wildly along the walls.

"You took your time in coming," I shout as I walk forward. "What kept you so long?"

Jack grins broadly when he sees me. "I knew you'd be fine, boy," he says. "Plenty of time for a cup of tea before we came looking." He pushes more rocks out of the way, wriggles through the hole and offers his hand.

I feel like throwing myself at Jack and hugging him. Instead I say, "I could've dug myself out easy, but then you wouldn't have had the chance to play the hero, so I had a nap instead."

Jack hits me playfully on the arm. "You hear that, boys?" he shouts back over his shoulder. "You been working beside a hero. Now hurry up and make that hole bigger so me and my pal can get out in time for dinner."

At that moment, standing beside my best friend and overwhelmed with gratitude and relief, I know I have made the right decision, Jack and I will go to war together.

CHAPTER 2

The Pyramids–November 1915

"Well, boy, did you ever think you'd see a sight like that?" Jack and I are standing in the hot desert sun, sweating under our uniforms, our heavy army boots sinking into the soft sand. I've just had my first ride on a camel, and now I'm staring up at one of the wonders of the world—the Great Pyramid of the pharaoh Cheops. "It beats scratching in some dark tunnel hundreds of feet under Coachman's Cove."

I nod in silent agreement, too awestruck to say anything. We've been in Egypt for weeks and I've almost got used to the noise, the bustle, the smells and the dust, but every day still throws up something magical

THE GREAT PYRAMID OF THE PHARAOH CHEOPS.

to astound me. Every corner we turn in Cairo presents a new and unexpected image—a donkey laden with gloriously bright carpets; a smiling old man pressing out hats on a filthy hand-cranked machine; a group of chattering women with only their dark eyes showing through their veils; rib-skinny dogs scrabbling in piles of garbage and apologetically crawling away from the kicks of passersby. It's a world so rich, varied and ancient that I doubt if I'll ever be able to go back to dull old Newfoundland.

I'd always known the pyramids were big—there was a picture on my schoolroom wall of these ancient monuments with dozens of tiny people scattered across the nearby desert—but knowing something from pictures and experiencing it for yourself are different. The base of the Great Pyramid stretches away for hundreds of feet on either side of me, and the slope appears to vanish up to heaven itself.

"Hard to believe it was built by men," I muse. "Each of those blocks must weight twenty or thirty tons."

"Obviously some Newfoundlander boys came over to give that old pharaoh a hand," Jack says with a grin.

"You want go inside?" Asim, the guide who brought us out here on the camels, is standing beside Jack. "I know best way. Show you King's Chamber. Ebo, my son, will watch camels."

I look around to the boy who rode out behind Asim; he's standing beside our camels, grinning broadly.

"*Shall* we go inside?" I ask Jack.

"Darn right, boy. We're miners from Coachman's Cove—it'll be a piece of cake. Maybe we'll even find some treasure."

Asim leads us around to the north side of the pyramid, past some raucous Australian soldiers who are organizing themselves for a photograph on the pyramid's slope. They yell greetings at us and we shout back and wave. Other soldiers are clambering around, some quite close to the top of the pyramid. Eventually, Asim turns and begins climbing.

We don't climb very high, maybe sixty or seventy feet, but it's exhausting work in the heat. The blocks are chest high and we have to drag ourselves up each level. I'm soaked in sweat and breathing heavily by the time we reach a small hole in the pyramid's side. It leads to a dark, downward-sloping passageway, barely waist high. Asim produces candles from inside his robe, lights them and crawls on his hands and knees into the passage. Jack follows and I bring up the rear.

It's pleasantly cool in the tunnel but hard going, crawling downhill on hands and knees while trying to keep my candle lit. I wish I had my old carbide lamp from the mine. Eventually, Jack and I move into a sort of a waddling crouch. It's awkward and hard on the knees, but we make better progress. After we've travelled about a hundred feet, Asim's flickering candle abruptly disappears. Jack exclaims in surprise, and I glimpse Asim's feet disappearing into a hole in the roof of the tunnel.

For a moment, I think it's some kind of trick and our guide has abandoned us, but then a candle is lowered and Asim's grinning face reappears.

"Now we go up," he says.

We haul ourselves through the hole in the roof and emerge in a tunnel the same size as the one we've just travelled through, but this one slopes up. We struggle along like sick crabs. My knees are close to giving out and I have hit my head on the ceiling of the tunnel at least a dozen times. Suddenly the space around us opens up into a large chamber.

"The Grand Gallery," Asim says, holding his candle as high as possible.

I can't touch the walls on either side, but in the candlelight, I can see that they come together in steps as they rise far above our heads.

"We could've used tunnels like this in the mines back home," I say.

"Right enough," Jack agrees. "It would've been much easier on the poor ponies."

We keep heading uphill along the gallery. It's a joy to walk upright, so I groan when we reach the end and have to duck down into another low passage. It's not long, though, and we're soon standing upright again.

"The King's Chamber," Asim informs us proudly.

We are in a long, narrow room with smooth walls. Jack and I hurry over to a large stone coffin in the middle. Peering in, I'm disappointed not to see the pharaoh's body.

"No treasure," Jack comments, glancing around at the bare walls and floor. "Someone beat us to it."

"Thieves," Asim explains. "Many, many years ago. All gone."

Jack shrugs in the flickering light. "Makes sense that they wouldn't leave treasure lying around for thousands of years just so a couple of boys from Newfoundland could see it." He scuffs his boot on the stone floor and raises a small cloud of dust. "Is this all?"

ot enough?" Asim replies.

enough," I say. The room's not spectacular, but I'm awed by the thought that I'm standing in the tomb of a man who died so long ago. The magnitude of where I am is overwhelming. I feel as if I'm deep underground, but I'm really more than a hundred feet above the sand. Everything below me, around me and for hundreds more feet above me has been built by people. When I think of the effort, time and organization required to move millions of huge blocks of stone into this incredible structure, I'm dumbfounded. "It's stunning," I say.

Asim seems satisfied with my expression of awe and rattles off a list of facts and figures about the pyramid and how it was built. Then he leads us back out.

The morning sun hurts my eyes as we emerge. Jack insists we scramble a bit higher to see the views before Asim shows us the two smaller pyramids and the Great Sphinx. Then we head back into town, tip Asim and his son generously, and go in search of something cold to drink.

"So now that you've seen the pyramids, what's left?" I ask Jack. We're sitting at an outdoor table beside the hospital where the wounded from the fighting in Gallipoli are being treated.

"Well, boy," Jack begins as he sips his drink, "I haven't quite seen enough flies yet."

I laugh. The flies have been driving us crazy during training, getting in our food and eternally buzzing around our heads. "And sand," I add. "A few more acres of sand would be nice. It's going to be a strange Christmas here with sand instead of snow."

"If we're still here," Jack says.

"What do you mean? Christmas is only a month away. Do you think we'll be in Gallipoli by then?"

"Maybe," Jack says, his voice serious. "But I was talking to an Aussie yesterday. He told me the story making the rounds is that them and the Kiwis are going to be evacuated from Gallipoli, and that means the Newfoundland boys will be as well. Seems the whole thing's a horrible botch-up. They were supposed to take the Turks by surprise, march up to Constantinople and knock Turkey out of the war. Instead they've spent six months clinging to godforsaken hillsides, launching hopeless attacks and trying desperately not to be pushed back into the Mediterranean. My Aussie friend was not complimentary or polite about the English generals who got them into this mess."

"There's always rumors of something going around. One week we're to march through Arabia, the next we're going to Greece."

"I think this one's different," Jack says. "I reckon even the generals have got the message at last—no one's going anywhere on Gallipoli. And you saw that hospital ship being unloaded last week. The casualties are horrible."

"Will they send us as reinforcements if everyone's going to be evacuated?"

Jack shakes his head. "It wouldn't make sense. But if I've learned one thing in this army, it's that orders don't have to make a lot of sense."

"That's true." I think of all the monotonous marching and pointless drills we've been doing over the past weeks. Life in the army isn't what I expected. Being in Cairo and seeing the pyramids *is* wonderful, but there's another side to our time here. Most days we're stuck in camp, filthy, hot, insect-bitten, sick, dog-tired and bored silly—and that's in the times between my urgent journeys to the latrines. Apart from watching the Aussies get into fights, there's not much excitement in camp. "If they don't send us to Gallipoli, where will we go?"

"Where the fighting is," Jack says. "France. That's where we can make a real difference."

I want to make a difference, but the thought of going to France doesn't thrill me. It'll just be more marching and drilling—except in wet, cold weather instead of sunshine. And the big battle at Loos in September bothers me. It was supposed to break the German defenses and let the cavalry through into open country, but it was a disaster. Despite using poison gas, the Allies had sixty thousand casualties. The number is horrifying. There are only about six hundred men in the whole

Newfoundland Regiment. What use can we be when sixty thousand men are killed or wounded in one battle? I feel hopeless, swamped by the numbers this war is throwing at me. My contribution is futile. What can one person do?

My gaze drifts across the street. Outside the hospital, there's a small garden where recovering soldiers can take the air and exercise. A few are out now, attended by nurses dressed in immaculate white uniforms. One, his face and eyes heavily bandaged, is being led gently around. Another, his right leg missing below the knee, struggles to master his new crutches. A third stands to one side, apparently uninjured but staring fixedly into the distance, completely oblivious to what's going on around him. A fourth sits in a wheelchair by the wrought-iron fence, a thick blanket pulled up to his neck despite the heat. He's not much older than me, and he's staring across at me and Jack. I wave but get no response.

"Poor sods," Jack says.

As we finish our drinks and stand to leave, I notice that the man in the chair is becoming agitated. He's throwing his head from side to side and seems to be struggling to stand. He must be tied in, because he's not making any progress. He keeps looking at me and mouthing something that I can't hear over the traffic passing along the road.

"Probably shell-shocked," Jack speculates.

Something about the struggling man fascinates me. I leave Jack and cross the street. As I approach, the man becomes even more agitated. A nurse has noticed and is advancing. The man throws himself to one side, almost tipping over the wheelchair. His blanket slips to the ground and the sight stops me in my tracks. He's not tied to his chair—he has no arms or legs. Only the bandaged stump of a right arm, ending above the elbow, jerks about helplessly. The man stares at me, a look of utter hatred distorting his face. "Damn you! Damn you!" he repeats over and over again.

The nurse has reached the man now. She's beautiful—olive-skinned with high cheekbones and dark almond eyes. I feel guilty about noticing her beauty. The contrast between her and the horror of the mutilated, angry, swearing man is shocking. Picking up the blanket, she calms him and tucks it in around him. Then she looks at me, smiles sadly and wheels her charge back toward the hospital. I watch her retreating back, partly awed by her beauty and partly disturbed by the hatred the maimed young man feels for me, simply because I'm whole.

Jack touches me on the shoulder. "Poor sod," he says again.

We turn and walk along the road.

"How did he survive injuries like that?" I ask.

"Maybe the injuries weren't too bad, but gangrene set in. I've heard the conditions of the hospital ships from Gallipoli aren't the best. Pity he survived."

"What do you mean?"

"He'd be better off dead," Jack says. "What sort of life does he have to look forward to? Helpless, unable to do anything for himself, needing care twenty-four hours a day. It's not a life I'd want."

We walk on in silence. Thinking about the mutilated soldier, I make a decision.

"Do you remember the Canadian kid we met on the ship over?" I ask.

"The boy from Saskatchewan who wanted to be a pilot?"

"Yeah, that's the one. Eddie, his name was. Maybe he had the right idea. This war's been going on for more than a year, and we don't seem to be any closer to winning it. Gallipoli, Loos—it's just disaster after disaster. For the tide to turn, it's going to take a lot of slogging and a lot more big battles—and a lot more men like those in the hospital."

"You having second thoughts about the army?"

"No. But perhaps the way to make a contribution is to do something other than be another soldier among thousands." I'm not certain where I'm going with this. I'm thinking it through as I talk.

"Like being a pilot?" Jack asks, a smile on his lips.

"Yes," I say, feeling slightly defensive. "Eddie says it's a wonderful feeling being up in the sky, and it must be better than marching nowhere in the heat and sand or sitting in a hole in the ground in France waiting for the next battle to happen."

"So you want to go up in those contraptions of string and canvas?"

I shrug. "Why not?"

Jack laughs out loud. "There's a problem with your wonderful new idea."

"What's that?" I ask, my voice rising in annoyance at Jack's negativity.

"You don't know the first thing about flying one of those things."

"I can learn," I respond sharply. "They must be training new pilots all the time. I'm going to apply for a transfer to fly aeroplanes."

"You're crazy, boy. You'd never get me up in one of those flying death traps. Only thing preventing you from going on a long fall with a short stop at the end is a few bits of wood and some canvas. Stay here with your mates. The others'll be back from Gallipoli soon enough. Then we'll be over in France to show the Kaiser what's what."

"At least falling from a plane would be a quick end." I'm annoyed at Jack for dismissing my ideas out of hand. "I'm going to request a transfer," I say firmly.

He nods and we fall silent again. I hadn't meant to say all that I did, but now that the idea's out, I can't ignore it. The more I think on it, the better it seems. I'll miss Jack and the other Newfoundlanders, but maybe I can get a transfer to Eddie's squadron.

The very next day, I go to see our company commander and ask for a transfer to the Royal Flying Corps.

CHAPTER 3

Down Instead of Up—December 1915

"Can you fly?" the officer demands.

"No, sir," I reply. "But I'm keen to learn."

My company commander approved my application for a transfer to the RFC, and two weeks before Christmas, I am reporting as ordered to a hotel room in Cairo. Despite the open windows and a ceiling fan turning sluggishly above, the room is oppressively hot. Sweat, from both the heat and my nervousness, streams down my sides beneath my uniform. The officer questioning me sits behind an ornately carved desk with my records in front of him. There's another officer in the room, sitting in an armchair in the far corner. He hasn't said anything, and his silent, watching presence makes me even more nervous.

"Any experience at all with aeroplanes?"

"No, sir."

"Ever driven any fast motor cars?"

"No, sir."

"Done any fox hunting?"

"No, sir."

"And you're from Newfoundland?"

"Yes, sir."

"Hmm." The officer perches a pair of half spectacles on his nose and thumbs through my records. The interview is not going well. "On the rifle range, you're no better than an average shot."

"Yes, sir," I say, although I'm not sure I was supposed to answer this.

The officer closes my file, removes his spectacles and looks up. "Why do you want to leave your friends and your regiment to join the RFC?"

"I want to contribute more to the war effort, sir."

"We all contribute in the best way we can," the officer says. "I'm certain that you Newfoundlanders will make a worthy contribution when you get over to France."

Now I know I'm going to be turned down.

"I admire your dedication and your attempt to help more, but with your background, I'm afraid I cannot recommend you for a position in the RFC."

I feel crushed. Over the past few days, the horribly crippled soldier has haunted my thoughts and I have placed a lot of hope in my application.

"Thank you, sir," I manage to choke out.

"Just a minute," mutters the man in the corner as I turn away. I stop and look over at him. "The RFC's not the only place a chap can make a greater contribution to the war effort."

"Sir?" I ask, confused.

The man stands up. He's tall, with a long, thin face, a hooked nose and a monocle in one eye. He speaks with an upper-class English accent. "I understand you were a miner back in Newfoundland?"

"Yes, sir."

"Familiar with explosives?"

"Yes, sir. I did my time at the face."

The man nods. He removes his monocle, polishes the lens with an immaculate white handkerchief and replaces it. "Ever been trapped underground?"

"Yes, sir. Once."

"How did you do?"

"I beg your pardon, sir?" The question confuses me.

"Were you scared?"

I think back to the moment of panic after the rock-fall. "At first, sir, but then I calmed down. The fall looked quite big, so there wasn't much I could do. I was in a space with enough air to last a long time and there was water running down the walls, so I just had to wait. As it turned out, they broke through to me quite quickly."

"I see," the man says. "You were alone?"

"Yes, sir."

He stares at me long enough for me to feel distinctly uncomfortable. Eventually, he declares, "Well, I think I should buy you a cup of tea."

Still confused, I follow the man out onto the street and into a tea shop. When we sit down, he introduces himself.

"My name's Griffin Ormsby-Smith." He pauses, apparently expecting me to say something. When I don't, he adds, "Of the Dublin Ormsby-Smiths." This also means nothing to me and all I can do is continue to stare blankly at the man. "Well, no matter," he goes on. "We made our money in the Rand gold mines in South Africa. That's where I grew up. Of course, I didn't do any mining myself—we had workers to do all that— but I did pick up a few things about the business, and that gave me an idea when the time came to do my bit in this present piece of unpleasantness."

It's strange to hear the war, which has taken hundreds of thousands of lives already, described as a "piece of unpleasantness." I'm beginning to wonder if this man is suffering from some form of shell-shock. I'm feeling miserable at being turned down for the RFC and less excited about tea with Ormsby-Smith by the minute.

"On December 20 last year, Indian troops were preparing to launch an attack outside Festubert, on the Western Front. They were weary, cold and wet, and they had been shelled heavily. In mid-morning, three mysterious flares went up from the German lines and a thousand yards of the Indian trenches disappeared in a series of massive explosions. The German assault troops walked through the front line unopposed and advanced hundreds of yards before they were stopped by a counter-attack. When our men recovered the old front lines, they found dugouts filled with soldiers— stone dead but without a mark on them."

Ormsby-Smith sips his tea and looks hard at me. I have no idea what he wants or why he has told me this tale, so I keep silent.

"Underground mines, you see," says Ormsby-Smith, as if that explains everything. "Not very big ones—but exploded all at once, they caused terrible damage and completely shocked the soldiers who survived. Imagine what mines, ten or twenty times the size of the ones at Festubert, might do."

I try to imagine, but I don't get very far before my companion tells me. "It would utterly destroy any defensive system and create a vast hole in the German lines. That would allow our troops to pour through into the open country behind the trenches, release the cavalry and roll up the Germans on either side. It would end the war."

Having made his point, Ormsby-Smith sits back, polishes his monocle once more and peers at me.

"I see," I say, even though I don't.

"Well?"

I'm obviously supposed to say more, but what? "It sounds like a wonderful idea," I offer.

"Yes, yes." Ormsby-Smith waves his monocle dismissively. "But do you want to be a part of it?"

"A part of it?" The more this man says, the more confused I get.

"The Germans are far ahead of us in the underground war. They haven't yet set off any really big mines, but it's only a matter of time before they come to the same conclusion I have." Ormsby-Smith is talking to me as if I'm a child. "We must do two things: find a way to stop the Germans from mining, and build our own systems to dig under the German trenches to place explosives there. Defense and attack, you see. I have been put in charge of creating units of tunnelers to do just that. You seem like just the sort of lad I could use. Do you want to be a tunneler? A miner? Someone who helps end the war? You said upstairs that you wanted to contribute more to the war effort. Well, here's your chance."

"I don't know," I say. I'm stunned and uncertain.

"Don't take too long making up your mind. I catch a boat back to France tomorrow. I'm offering you important work, and we're looking for as many experienced miners as we can find." Ormsby-Smith screws his monocle back into his eye. "The pay's six shillings a day."

"Six shillings a day?" That's got my attention. It's six times what I'm earning as a regular soldier. An image of my dad sitting by the fire back in Coachman's Cove, silently cursing his crushed leg and

CAP BADGE FOR THE ROYAL ENGINEERS.

his inability to earn a wage for his family, flashes into my head. I see my mom behind him, wringing her work-reddened hands on her apron, her face creased with worry. What I could send home from six shillings a day would make a huge difference to their lives. "I'll do it," I say impulsively.

"Excellent, excellent. Good man." Ormsby-Smith stands up. "I'll clear it with your commanding officer. Be at the docks with your kit by nine o'clock tomorrow morning. We'll have you in France by Christmas." He turns and strides off.

"Thank you, sir," I call after him. He gives me a vague wave over his shoulder.

What have I done? I came here to try to be a pilot flying in the clear air above the trenches. Now I'm going to be a miner in dark tunnels below the trenches. The money's good, but it will mean saying good-bye to Jack and not joining my Newfoundland comrades when they return from Gallipoli. I feel horribly confused. I thought I had left Newfoundland behind to experience adventure and see the world, but the simple mention of six shillings a day has brought home rushing back to me and has returned me to my life underground.

I leave the tearoom and step back out into the noise and bustle of the Cairo streets. What a strange war this is turning out to be.

CHAPTER 4

Meeting the Moles—Christmas 1915

"Welcome to the Moles," the officer shouts cheerfully as I jump down from the back of the ammunition wagon that has brought me on the final leg of my journey to this farm on the Somme River. It's evening after a long, uncomfortable day, and this is the headquarters of 169 Tunnelling Company. There's a steady cold rain falling from a leaden gray sky, and it's Christmas Eve. I miss the Egyptian sun already. I had expected a period of training after I arrived in France, but I was immediately shuttled north to the town of Albert on a succession of trains, trucks and wagons that had nothing in common but their slowness and lack of comfort.

I snap to attention and salute. "Thank you, sir."

"Oh, we Moles don't stand on formality here," says the officer, stepping forward and offering his hand for me to shake. "Of course, if the brass is around, we must put on a show. But between us, we're here to get a job done—not to stand guard at the palace. Name's Captain Reginald Philpot, but most call me Reggie, or worse behind my back, I daresay. You must be Alec Shorecross."

"I am, sir," I say, shaking Philpot's hand.

"Excellent. You're a hard-rock man, I hear."

"Yes, sir. I worked the Terra Nova copper mine at Coachman's Cove in Newfoundland."

"Never made it out that way," Philpot says as he leads me toward a large barn. "Closest I got was Sudbury. I was a mining surveyor with the International Nickel Company. Good to have someone who understands real rocks. It's all chalk hereabouts, which isn't too bad. Up by Ypres it's mostly clay—foul stuff to work in—or else sand that's so waterlogged it's like digging in porridge." He shakes his head. "Anyway, you're our first Newfoundlander. There's 274 of us in the 169th—mostly English from the coal mines in the north, although there's a few from the sewer and train tunnels under London. The rest are a motley crew: couple of Canadians, handful of Irish, few dozen Scots and Welsh. Good chaps for the most part, if they don't have too much to drink and get into a fight."

SOLDIERS IN THEIR BARN.

Two men trudge round the corner of the ramshackle farmhouse. They're an odd-looking pair: one is tall for a miner and skinny, with strands of dirty red hair poking out from beneath his soft cloth cap; the other is short and tubby and dark-haired. Both are dressed in heavy canvas pants and wool sweaters, and covered in light gray dirt. They carry short picks over their shoulders.

"Hello, Ewan, Bernie," Philpot shouts. "Any activity?"

The taller man's reply is drowned out by an immense explosion that shakes the ground behind me. I jump and turn around.

"That's only Irma," Philpot says. "She's our very own 9.2-inch Howitzer. The artillery boys dug her in a couple of days ago. She can lob a three-hundred-pound shell almost six miles, but she does make a terrible fuss about it."

"Fritz is still scratching away," says the redhead as he draws nearer, "but he's getting closer."

"We'll need to keep listening, then," Philpot replies. "Meet our new Mole, Alec. He's a hard-rock man all the way from the colony of Newfoundland."

I step forward and offer my hand.

"Pleased to meet you," the taller man says. "Name's Ewan Gunn, and this is Bernie Davidson. He's a Geordie, from Newcastle, but don't hold that against him."

"And don't listen to nowt this Scottish streak o' misery says," the shorter man adds as we shake. I struggle to understand his heavy accent. "I'm for scraping some o' this grime off." He strolls off toward the barn.

"Who's on shift now?" Philpot asks Ewan.

"Lieutenant Harrington's crew."

"Excellent," Philpot replies. "I want to take Alec on a tour of the workings, and he'll be joining Harrington's crew."

Ewan scratches his face thoughtfully, leaving pale streaks in the dirt on his cheek. "I heard that the boys in 185 Company have started a deep tunnel toward La Boisselle. That true?"

"Indeed it is," Philpot says. "The plan is to place some deep mines under Fritz in time for the big attack next summer."

Ewan's face creases into a lopsided grin. "So the war isn't going to be over by Christmas? Pity, I was looking forward to going home tomorrow."

Philpot laughs. "You won't be going home for this Christmas. Want to put a fiver on next year?"

Ewan rubs his chin with exaggerated thoughtfulness. "If they make the mine big enough, we can blow up the German lines next summer, mount our cavalry horses and ride straight to Berlin."

"And if that fails," Philpot adds, "we'll just keep tunneling until we reach Berlin and put a large charge under the Kaiser."

Ewan furrows his brow in concentration. "Must be five hundred miles or so to Berlin as the crow flies. There's 5,280 feet in a mile, and in good ground we can tunnel twenty-five feet a day." He closes his eyes and moves his lips in silent calculation. "So if nothing goes wrong and we don't take any leave, I reckon we'll be under Berlin in about three hundred years. I think I'll hang on to my fiver."

"Smart man," Philpot says, laughing. "You can always see the advantage of a good education."

I listen in silence to the banter between the two men. Their light-hearted exchange is nothing like the formal behavior I've become used to in the army. It makes me think I'll enjoy working with the Moles.

"All right if we go into town tonight?" Ewan's question interrupts my train of thought.

"Might as well," Philpot says. "But before you go, can you show Alec where to bed down?"

"Sure." Ewan nods at me, shifts his pick to the opposite shoulder and strolls toward the barn.

"Thank you, sir," I say, turning to Philpot.

"I'll meet you out here when you've got your kit stowed," he replies. "And less of the 'sir.'"

I pick up my kit bag, sling it over my shoulder then turn to follow after Ewan.

"You're from Newfoundland, then," he says over his shoulder. His voice is soft and lilting—Highland Scots, I guess. "I've a cousin lives in St. John's. Name's Hamish. His family moved out when he was a wee one. They were fisher folk from the Isle of Skye, so that's what they took up over there. He joined up first weeks. Received a postcard from him from Gallipoli."

"I was over in Egypt," I say. "Word is that the Newfoundlanders are being evacuated and brought over to France."

"That right? Perhaps I'll see Hamish soon enough, then."

We've reached the barn. There are paper chains and strips of colored paper around the door, and above it all a sign that reads "Merry Christmas." Ewan places his pick by the door and leads me inside. The barn is crammed with bunks, three high and two deep. There must be beds for a couple of hundred men in here.

"Your timing's good," Ewan tells me. "There's usually no space in here and newcomers are put in tents, but a couple of men were wounded yesterday, so their bunks are free."

"What happened? Was there a cave-in?"

"No, a random shell caught them as they were heading back from the line. One chap lost a leg." Ewan indicates an empty space on the bottom layer of a tier.

"Aren't you worried about a shell hitting the barn?" I ask.

"It's possible—especially if Fritz is trying to zero in on Irma—but it's all long-range stuff. We're a good two and a half miles from Fritz's lines. We could be unlucky, but at least we'll be a lot more comfortable in our last days than those poor sods in the front lines, huddled in holes dug into the sides of trenches." Ewan grins at me. "I'll let you stow your kit and then Reggie'll show you around."

I spread out my kit, and sit for a moment on the edge of my bunk. I'm a bit stunned by how different life as a Mole seems to be. It's not like the life of a soldier I've become used to, it seems much more relaxed and informal. Perhaps going back to being a miner won't be so bad after all.

I head back out into the rain and find Captain Philpot standing beside a narrow-gauge railway. Behind him is a flatbed carriage loaded with lengths of timber, but instead of a steam engine, there's a bored-looking horse harnessed to the front.

"Too close to the front to use engines in daylight," the captain explains when he sees my look. "Fritz keeps an eye on us all the time and he'd spot the smoke from the engine." He waves vaguely at the dark shapes of half a dozen observation balloons floating over the German lines. "Most work's done at night anyway, but we use Dobbin here for small loads during the day. Thought we'd hitch a ride."

We climb up, seat ourselves on the timbers and set off at a walking pace. A soldier walks by the horse's head, but I suspect the beast would simply plod along even without anyone to guide it. I keep glancing at the balloons, nervous that there might be a German observer in one, looking at me through binoculars and calling our coordinates to the artillery.

At first the landscape is busy with activity: wagons heading in all directions, soldiers marching back and forth, field kitchens cooking up rations. As we progress, though, the activity diminishes, but I'm surprised to see French peasants working their late-season crops as if there were no war on. After about half an hour, the railway ends at the edge of a small wood.

"We walk from here," Philpot says, jumping down.

We are already completely soaked through from the rain, but it is still a relief to enter the shelter of the trees. Partway through the wood, the path we're following becomes a shallow trench that deepens gradually until we can walk upright. Suddenly, the world we have been passing through is confined to a couple of sandbagged walls a foot or two away on either side. We squeeze past messengers and ration parties moving in the opposite direction, and pass the dark entrances to crude dugouts. Wider sections of the trench contain stacked supplies, empty sandbags, tools and rolls of barbed wire. Eventually, we come to a cross trench and Philpot turns right.

"This is the third line," he says. "It's where we begin the tunnels."

"Wouldn't the distance to the German front lines be shorter if the tunnels began in our front line?" I ask.

"Shorter, yes, but there are two reasons we don't do that. First, we're out of German mortar range here, so Fritz can't lob a bomb over and close a tunnel entrance. Second, we run a sloping shaft—it helps with air circulation and the removal of the chalk waste—so we have to start farther back to get deep enough. We have a few vertical shafts that start from the front lines—took them over from the French earlier in the year—but they're more trouble than they're worth. Besides, we're just digging defensive tunnels at the moment, not trying to get all the way over to Fritz's lines. He's been tunneling here for a lot longer than we have, so our main task is to find his tunnels and blow them before he can set off a really big mine."

We come to what looks like another dugout entrance. Philpot grabs a couple of candles from a box set into the trench wall, lights them and hands me one. We duck through the entrance into a gently sloping tunnel. After about twenty feet, it widens out into a small wood-lined room. A soldier is pumping a large pair of bellows with a steady rhythm. He looks bored. A pipe runs from the bellows into another tunnel in the opposite wall. Philpot nods to the soldier and we continue.

The next section of tunnel is five feet high and three wide, almost tall enough to stand upright and wide enough for two people to pass. At first the roof, floor and walls are wood, but as we descend the beams are farther apart and the walls become pale rock. The floor is cut in shallow steps and the air pipe from the bellows at the entrance runs down one side. Everything is damp and I have to concentrate to keep my footing.

Eventually, the tunnel dries out and we come to a transverse tunnel, running to the right and left.

"We've just passed under our front lines," Philpot says as we turn left. "If you were twenty-five feet higher, you'd be in no-man's-land and probably dead."

It feels odd to be walking underground, relatively safe from the enemy, while a war goes on above our heads.

"This transverse tunnel runs parallel to the front line, and other tunnels run from it toward Fritz's lines," explains Philpot as we reach a side tunnel on our right. "The chalk's so hard that it's very difficult to dig through it quietly. These are defensive tunnels, dug so that we can find Fritz's tunnels before he has a chance to excavate a chamber and place a mine under our trenches. We're always trying to extend them, but mostly we sit and listen for Fritz and try to work out what he's doing. If we think he's getting too close, we try to set a camouflet to blow in his tunnel."

"Camouflet?"

"A small mine that we use to try and blow up one of Fritz's tunnels. Sometimes it's a small cave, sometimes just a drilled hole, filled with explosives. It depends how close we think Fritz is. Ideally we want to destroy the German tunnel and catch their miners working in it. Of course, they're trying to do the same to us."

As we talk, we move along the tunnel toward the German front line. Soon we reach a group of three men. One is attacking the face of the tunnel with a short pick, chipping off lumps that his companion is loading into sandbags. The third man is farther back. He's an officer and has a stethoscope-like instrument hanging around his neck.

"Evening, Harrington," Philpot says. "I've brought a new boy down to have a look. Anything interesting going on?"

"Hello, Reggie. No, not much." He turns to me and offers his hand. "My name's Harrington. You'll be joining my squad, so this is what you can look forward to." He waves in the direction of the digger at the face.

"My name's Alec Shorecross, sir," I say. "Is all the work here by hand?" I can't help thinking how much faster things would go if they used the blasting patterns we had back home.

"Has to be," Harrington says. "Partly to prevent gas buildup. The ventilation system's not the best, and an explosion leaves a lot of carbon monoxide. It can collect in the rock fractures and cavities, seep into the tunnels, and kill you before you know it. We also need to keep as quiet as possible—sound travels a long way through chalk. Have a listen through the geophone and see what you can hear."

Harrington passes me the device from around his neck and orders the men at the face to stop working.

I place the ends in my ears and the round detector against the chalk, close my eyes and concentrate. At first I can't hear anything, but then I begin to pick up a soft scratching sound. At first I think it must be a small animal of some sort, but as I listen a picture forms in my mind. I see a soldier crouching at a rock face, rhythmically scraping and digging at the chalk—a soldier in a German uniform. Now that I know what it is, the noise sounds much louder.

I tear the geophone out of my ears. "I can hear Germans digging, sir. Close by. We have to get out." I fight to control the panic in my voice. My mind has conjured a pick breaking through the wall before me, followed quickly by a German soldier with a rifle and bayonet.

Harrington laughs. "You have good ears, Shorecross, but we're not in any danger. The sound you hear is coming from forty or fifty feet away, and they probably have a man with a geophone there listening to us. As long as we can hear each other, we're both safe. It's a longish silence that's dangerous. That means the other side has stopped digging and laid a charge. That's the time to get out."

"Sorry, sir," I say, feeling sheepish.

"Don't be," Harrington reassures me. "I'm impressed that you could pick up the sounds so quickly. I think you'll fit in well with the squad."

As Captain Philpot and I return along the tunnel, I wonder about this new world I have entered. I had assumed that mining would be a safe occupation—away from the shells and machine guns—but now, with images of dark explosions and violent fights in tunnels dancing round my brain, I'm not so sure.

As we emerge back into the trench, Philpot checks his watch. "Midnight," he says. "Merry Christmas."

CHAPTER 5

Listening—February 1916

"Fritz is getting close to tunnel number 3," Harrington says. We're sitting on a couple of camp chairs outside the barn, waiting for our turn to go underground. It's a chilly February day, but the weak sun is making a brave attempt to force its way through a veil of high cloud. "We'll need to keep a close watch on him. I want you to take over listening duties on our shift."

"Do you think I'm ready?" I ask. I've been doing a bit of everything since I joined the Moles, but Harrington thinks I have a good ear and he's been giving me more and more listening work lately.

"I do. You can distinguish the different tools Fritz uses, and you're getting to be a decent judge of how far off he's working. Besides, the tunnels toward La Boisselle are being pushed ahead rapidly, and word is we're to start a big attack tunnel under the ridge by Beaumont-Hamel. Our resources are spread thin and I need good listeners like you to make sure we keep Fritz under control."

I nod agreement, although it's frightening to think that I will be the man who's responsible for getting everyone out before the Germans blow a camouflet.

"As far as I can tell, Fritz is still about twenty feet away on the same level as our listening tunnel. He knows we're there, so it'll be a race. You'll listen all the time in the post we've carved back from the mining face, and I'll have our diggers stop work for ten minutes every hour so you can get a clear listen to Fritz. It'll mean long shifts, but we've little choice at this point."

"I'll do my best." Of course I say this, but will my best be good enough? There are lives at stake, and I am daunted by the thought.

Working in the underground darkness is hour after hour of mind-numbing boredom, and listening duties are the worst. Keeping your concentration at a level high enough to recognize the faint noises coming through the geophones—even when you know that subtle changes in those noises can mean the difference between life and death—is immensely hard. There have been times when my head has suddenly jerked up and I've been faced with the sick realization that I've dozed off.

"We should make a start if we're to reach the tunnel in time." Harrington stretches and looks up at the gray sky. There's a two-seater observation plane heading east to the German lines. I can just hear the coarse thump of its engine. The lieutenant stands and I follow. "I'll round up the boys and you get the listening gear together."

"Okay," I say, heading for the equipment shed beside the barn, my head filled with thoughts of my new responsibility.

As usual, the journey to the front lines is uneventful. The reason for the lack of activity on this section of the front was revealed a few days ago, when the Germans launched a massive assault to the south of us. All eyes are on Verdun now, and we Moles underground seem to be the only ones fighting the war around here.

"D'you think Fritz'll break through the Frenchies at Verdun?" Bernie asks as we rumble toward the trenches on our light railway wagon.

"He'd better not," Ewan replies. "If he does, he'll head for Paris—and that means he'll be behind us. Then our only option'll be to cut and run for the Channel ports."

"Maybe the war *will* be over by this Christmas," I suggest, remembering Ewan and Philpot's friendly bet.

"Aye," Bernie says, "but wi' the wrong side winning."

We sit silently contemplating that possibility. None of us wants the Germans to win, but we do want the war to end.

Staring hard at the side of my head, Ewan breaks the silence by saying, "What d'you reckon, Bernie? Are they getting bigger?"

I self-consciously lift my hand to where Ewan is looking, trying to work out what he means.

"Aye." Bernie nods. "You're right enough there, Ewan."

"What?" I ask, feeling the first twinges of worry. "What are you talking about?"

"Your ears, man," Bernie says. "They're getting bigger."

"They are that," Ewan agrees. "Sign of a good listening Mole."

I instinctively feel my ears to see if they have grown before I realize I'm being teased. Ewan and Bernie are still chuckling when we dismount the railcar and head down into the trench.

Once in the tunnel, I settle myself as comfortably as possible in the cramped listening post. Ewan and Bernie go on to the face with a final whispered comment about my ears. They move slowly and silently, their boots muffled with rags. I've known them only a short while and they're constantly teasing me, but working together underground creates a bond and the three of us have become close friends. I take a deep breath, place the end of the listening device against the chalk and close my eyes.

At first there's a confusion of sound, but as I focus I begin to distinguish different activities. There's the soft, drawn-out scrape of Ewan and Bernie working nearby. They're prying off lumps of chalk by hand and placing them in sandbags. I can even hear the filled bags being dragged back along the tunnel. The distant thump is an exploding shell. The sharp, regular sounds are the Germans working at the face of their own tunnel. They're still using picks, and as Harrington said, they sound about twenty feet away. No need to worry as long as I can hear them working and they don't get close enough to break through.

As planned, our diggers fall completely silent after an hour. I strain to listen. Individual pick blows are now clear. To a good listener, the noise of a pick is like a signature. Some German miners take long swings and deliver hard blows, while others work with a short chipping motion. Each man is different. I'm not that good yet, although the man I'm listening to has a very regular rhythm.

I can even hear distant voices. I can recognize the guttural tone of German, but I can't make out the words. Suddenly a cough sounds very close. I concentrate hard, but it's not repeated. I wonder if it's Ewan or Bernie. The chalk and the fractures in it can distort things, magnifying some sounds and muffling others to make it difficult to determine distance. After ten minutes, our crew begins work again.

The hours pass and above me day turns to night. Under cover of darkness, work begins in the trenches and no-man's-land. New noises intrude into my narrow world—the scrape of shovels reinforcing a trench wall, the ping of hammers repairing barbed wire, even the occasional harsh scuffle of hobnailed boots moving over duckboards in the bottom of the trenches. I acknowledge the new noises and continue to focus on the steady rhythm of the German picks.

Boredom begins to weigh upon me. At least on the surface, the soldiers are busy and moving about. I have to sit, crammed into my narrow scrape in the wall, not moving and controlling my breathing. My only reality is the soft pick, pick, pick of the enemy working twenty feet away. The rhythm lulls me. I think back to the plane I saw overhead that morning, and that leads to memories of Eddie, the Canadian I met on the boat over. I wonder if he's around here somewhere, pursuing his dreams of flight. I wrote to him but haven't heard anything back.

My thoughts drift to Jack. The Newfoundland Regiment evacuated from Gallipoli, so they should be in France soon. Then I'll look him up and see how he's doing. Unexpectedly, a third figure drifts into my mind—the nurse from the hospital in Cairo. In my mind's eye, I see the angry soldier without arms or legs and feel a surge of pity, but his image is soon replaced by the nurse's sad, dark eyes. I wonder if she's still in Egypt, or if the hospital will be moved to France with the men from Gallipoli. I imagine looking her up, but how would I find her? I don't even know her name.

I shake my head and haul my attention back to the present. Something's wrong. I push everything else out of my mind and concentrate on the noise of the German pick. It's the same as before, regular and twenty feet away.

A soft tap on my shoulder almost gives me a heart attack.

"Any change?" Harrington whispers in my ear.

I shake my head. "Still about twenty feet away," I mouth.

Harrington's brow furrows in puzzlement. "They're not making any progress," he says. "What are they up to?"

"Could be digging out a chamber to pack with explosives," I suggest.

"Odd they should do that out here. They haven't reached our lines yet." He looks truly bewildered. "Well, keep listening. If the picking stops, you should hear them dragging the explosives into the chamber. That's when we'll set off our camouflet to collapse their tunnel."

I nod again as the lieutenant moves to check on Ewan and Bernie at the face. I strain to hear any change in the noises from the enemy tunnel. The monotonous pick, pick, pick continues without a break. Whoever is working there is an extraordinary man, maintaining such a steady pace and never seeming to tire. And yet, he doesn't seem to progress either.

"Raus hier! Schnell!"

It takes me a moment to realize that I am hearing clear German words very close. Is it a quirk of the surrounding rock that makes them sound as close as the cough I heard earlier?

Schnell. I know that means "quickly." *Raus,* I've also heard before. I think it means "out." Is this someone telling people to get out quickly? I listen hard, but all I hear is the rhythmic chipping of the pick twenty feet away.

A cold shiver runs down my spine as I realize what's been bothering me: the noise is *too* regular. I've been tricked. It's a trap. The pick, pick, pick isn't moving because it's not an incredibly disciplined man digging through the chalk—it's a machine tapping out a tune to distract me from the work going on much closer. The spot where a man coughed earlier and now everyone is being ordered to get out quickly because the camouflet is ready.

I turn to shout a warning to Harrington, Ewan and

Bernie at the face, but my first word is drowned out by a thunderous explosion. A dust-filled hot wind races up the tunnel like a huge fist, forcing me back into my listening post. All the air is sucked out of my lungs, leaving me gasping. My candle blows out and I'm plunged into darkness.

Gradually the roaring in my ears subsides and I choke in a deep breath of dusty air, harsh with the smell of explosives. Coughing painfully, I feel my way into the tunnel and toward the working face. I'm stopped a few feet along by rubble that blocks the way. The German camouflet has caved in our workings, trapping or killing Harrington, Ewan and Bernie. A tidal wave of guilt surges over me—this is my fault for not working out what was going on. I push the feeling back down—there'll be plenty of time for guilt later—and desperately begin digging where the rubble feels loosest.

The fall is unstable and the chalk collapses almost as fast as I can haul it away. Where's the rescue team? They must have heard the explosion. The dust and the acrid smell of explosives tear at my throat. I have a pounding headache, caused by gas from the explosion. But I keep going. I have to.

"I'm coming," I shout as I claw wildly at the rubble. Then I feel a hand. I grasp it hard, praying that it's attached to a living body. To my immense relief, the hand squeezes back.

"Alec?" Harrington's voice asks.

"I'm coming," I repeat. We both work until there's a hole between us; it's narrow and unstable but a connection nonetheless. "I'll pull you through," I say as I work to enlarge the hole.

"No." Harrington sounds calm. "Gas."

I shudder at the thought of the odorless, tasteless poison collecting in the air around me. "You have to come out," I urge.

"No," he repeats. "Bernie . . . legs trapped. Ewan . . . unconscious." He's having trouble breathing and his words come in short, unconnected spurts. "Ewan first . . . I'll push . . . you pull."

Working by feel in the darkness, I find Ewan's arms and haul with all my might. It's a tight squeeze and there's chalk falling all around us, but at last he's through. The hole is narrowing as more rocks fall. I'm dizzy and have the uncomfortable sense that the world is tilting around me. I try to enlarge the hole.

"No," Harrington orders.

"But I can get you out," I protest.

"I'll dig Bernie . . . you get Ewan . . . fresh air."

"The walls are crumbling," I gasp. I'm groggy and have trouble finding words and stringing them together coherently. "You must come now. It's your only chance."

"It's an order." I hear Harrington sucking in several rasping breaths. With an effort I can hear in his voice, he shouts, "Bernie . . . one of my men . . . I do not leave my men behind. Go!"

As I hesitate, a large piece of chalk falls from the roof beside me. I find Ewan's shoulders and begin hauling him back along the tunnel. I barely know where I am and keep staggering painfully against the walls. My legs feel like water and the ground seems to be moving of its own accord. I'm weak and nauseous, and my head feels as if someone's beating on it with a hammer. Ewan's a dead weight that I can move along only an inch at a time. The gas is thickening. I can see lights dancing in front of my eyes. I can't go any farther. I sit down heavily on the tunnel floor and watch as beams of light skitter across the walls around me. They're beautiful, painting dazzling patterns on the chalk. I stare at them in wonder. If this is death, it's exquisite.

Just then, hands grasp me roughly under the shoulders. I twist my head to look around. The tunnel is full of hunched, unearthly creatures with no faces.

"I've got you, lad," a voice says. The voice is strangely muffled, but it's undoubtedly human. The figures aren't monsters from my gas-addled brain but men wearing respirator masks. "We'll get you and your mate out."

"Harrington . . . Bernie," I mumble. I try to point back down the tunnel, but my arm doesn't seem to work and simply flops stupidly down beside me.

"We'll get them too. Don't you worry."

The voice is calm and reassuring. I want to go to sleep. My last feeling before I slip into unconsciousness is disappointment. The delightful, magical dancing lights are just the beams of the torches carried by the rescue crew.

RESPIRATOR MASKS.

CHAPTER 6

Hospital—March 1916

The journey to the hospital was a nightmare. Jumbled images tumble over each other in my head. I remember being thrown over someone's shoulder, trying to focus on the ground as it rushed past below me, and the bile from my stomach tearing agonizingly at my raw throat as I vomit. I bounced around in an ambulance or a truck, surrounded by the screams of wounded men. I was left outside, staring up at puffy clouds drifting magically in a delicate blue sky. At one point I was dragged back from my dreams by a wonderful cool cloth on my forehead and a soothing, gentle voice, but maybe that was just another dream.

"You're a very lucky man." There's a doctor standing beside my cot.

"Am I dead?" I ask. It's a stupid question, but it seems important. My throat hurts.

"No," the doctor says with a smile. "You and your friend just breathed in too much carbon monoxide."

"Ewan?"

"He'll be fine as well. You'll both have nausea, headaches and dizziness for a few days, but with rest and fresh air, you should be right as rain in a week or two."

I want to ask about the other two men at the tunnel face. I know I tried to dig them out, but I can't remember their names. "The others?" I croak.

"Only you two were brought in. Were there others in the tunnel?"

I nod, and immediately regret it as pain pounds in my head.

"Try to keep as still as possible," the doctor says. "The headaches will pass. And try to rest. I'll send the nurse over with something to help you sleep."

I grunt what I hope sounds like a thank-you. After the doctor leaves, I move my head very slowly to look around. I'm in a row of cots along one wall of a large tent. There's a matching row along the other side, all full with bandaged forms. The flaps at either end of the tent are open, and as I stare at one of them, a nurse

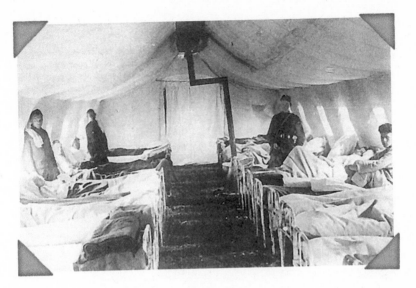

A MILITARY HOSPITAL.

steps inside and looks around. Her gaze settles on me, and she smiles and moves forward.

Either I'm dreaming or it's the nurse from Egypt. Without thinking, I sit up. The hospital tent lurches sickeningly. The walls distort and swirl around me, and I feel as if I'm falling. I reach out wildly to try to steady myself, but there's nothing to grab and I collapse over the side of my cot, retching violently.

Gentle hands move me back onto my pillow, and a damp cloth wipes my mouth and chin.

"Do not be silly," an angelic voice says in heavily accented English. "You must stay still and rest. Take this."

I desperately want to see who's talking, but I'm terrified to open my eyes. I feel a pill being placed on my tongue and water dribbled into my mouth.

"Swallow this," the voice says. "It will help you sleep."

I swallow and open my eyes. I still feel dizzy, but my surroundings appear to be fairly stable. I'm staring at the nurse from Cairo. "Egypt," I say.

The nurse looks confused. "Rest," she says, and I feel a wonderfully cool cloth on my forehead. With a sigh, I close my eyes and sleep.

When I wake up, Captain Philpot is beside my bed. "Good morning," he says cheerfully.

I try to reply, but my mouth feels full of sand. Philpot gently lifts my head and dribbles water into my mouth. It helps.

While I try to gather my confused thoughts, Philpot chatters on. "Thought I should come down and see how you two were doing. You got a nasty dose of gas. So did Ewan, but he seems to be better than you—maybe because he was unconscious and not breathing deeply. You were working hard."

"The others?" I ask. At least my throat feels a bit better.

"Gone, I'm afraid," Philpot says. "Bernie was trapped by the fall and Harrington refused to leave him, even though he had a chance. The pressure in the chalk was too great and the hole closed up. When the rescue crew finally got through, four days later, Bernie and Harrington were both dead. I've recommended Harrington for a medal."

I lie silent, absorbing the news. I feel strangely detached from what the captain has told me. I was fond of Harrington and Bernie was my friend, but the news of their deaths doesn't trigger any emotion except guilt at not caring. Will I always be like this, numb and indifferent? Then something Philpot said surfaces through the cotton wool that seems to be wrapped around my brain.

"It took *four* days to dig Bernie and Harrington out?"

"It did."

"How long have I been in here?"

"A week. The doctor said he was worried that you'd never wake up. He says it'll be a few days before you're out of bed, and several weeks before you can be back with us. But you should make a full recovery."

A week of my life and I can remember nothing but a few isolated incidents—and I'm not even sure those were real. I want to talk, but I can't seem to think of anything to say. My brain is incredibly sluggish.

I sense a figure arriving at the opposite side of my bed from Philpot. A voice from one of my dreams says, "I think we should let our patient rest now, Captain."

"Of course," Philpot says as he stands up. "Get plenty of rest, Shorecross, and do exactly what this lovely young lady tells you." With a nod, he turns and heads out of the hospital tent.

I gently turn my head, although I know who I'm going to see. "Egypt," I say.

The nurse nods. "I remember where I saw you. The poor soldier in Cairo shouted at you."

"Yes." I desperately want to say something else, but my brain won't come up with anything. I furrow my brow in concentration.

"What is wrong?" the nurse asks.

A word rises through my brain like a bubble in maple syrup. "Name," I manage to murmur.

The nurse smiles. "My name is Manon Wouters." She pronounces her surname like *Vooters*. "I am from Flanders, in Belgium."

"Alec," I reply weakly.

"I know. Alec Shorecross. It is on the chart at the foot of your bed."

Again that smile. It's the only thing that seems real in this strange world where I find myself.

"So you're finally awake."

I blink and focus on the figure behind Manon. Ewan, dressed in a hospital gown and leaning on a cane. I feel vaguely annoyed that he's here. I simply wanted to lie back and stare at Manon.

"I came to thank you," Ewan goes on. "You saved my life in that tunnel."

There's something I should say here, but it won't come. I try to smile, but I think it comes out more as a grimace.

"We should let Alec rest," Manon says, and I feel a surge of jealousy that the "we" includes Ewan and not me. I should say something, or else Manon will leave with Ewan and I'll never see her again. But what can I say?

I open my mouth. "I love you."

Manon looks startled.

Ewan grins. "My pal Alec's a fast worker," he says.

I feel my face blush with embarrassment, but Manon doesn't seem to mind now that she has got over her surprise.

"I think you need to rest," she says. Then she leans over and plants a kiss on my forehead. It's the lightest of brushes, but my skin feels on fire.

I watch as she helps Ewan back to his cot. I feel unutterably stupid, but as I drift into sleep, I'm happier than I have been in a long time.

CHAPTER 7

Recovery and Loss—March 1916

The late March sun is only a slightly brighter patch through the high cloud, but it's the first day without rain since I've been able to get about and I'm enjoying sitting on the veranda, heavily wrapped in blankets. My recovery has been slower than I expected and I have been moved for recuperation from the tent to the abandoned French villa that dominates the hospital grounds.

Ewan has recovered more quickly and left to rejoin the Moles three days ago. My headaches have almost gone and I get dizzy only if I twist my head a certain way or stand up too quickly. The doctor says another

RECOVERING ON THE HOSPITAL GROUNDS.

week and I'll be ready to rejoin my unit. That's fine by me—it means a few more days with Manon. I've got over my embarrassment at blurting out, "I love you," but I've come to realize that I meant it.

My weeks of recovery have been a wonderful dream come true. I have seen Manon every day. She fed me when I was too weak to feed myself, talked gently to me when I was confused and pushed my wheelchair along the villa's corridors when it was too wet to go into the garden. I admire her tremendously. She escaped Belgium after the Germans invaded and joined the British army as a nurse. She had to abandon everything when she fled—her home, her country and her family— and the only time her face darkens with anger is when she talks about watching the line of spike-helmeted soldiers tramping along the cobbled roads of her quiet and peaceful village.

"Well, Alec, are you enjoying our wonderful sunshine?" I look up to see Manon's smiling face.

"It's all the better now that you're here," I say. It's a corny line, but I can't seem to help saying dumb things when Manon's around. Fortunately, she doesn't appear to mind.

"Are all the Newfoundlanders such smooth talkers?" she asks with a laugh that sends shivers down my spine.

"I'm the best," I say. I have decided to tell Manon how I feel about her before I go back to the war, but the right moment hasn't presented itself. Perhaps today it will. "Shall we take a walk around the garden?"

"Why not?"

Manon helps me stand and takes my arm as I go down the veranda steps. I could manage on my own, but I'm not about to complain that this beautiful girl is close beside me with her arm locked in mine.

"I think you pretend to be less well than you are," she says teasingly.

"If it weren't for you," I say, "I'd be at death's door."

Manon punches me playfully on the arm. We walk in silence for a moment and I notice Manon's smile fade. "Is something wrong?" I ask.

"I received a letter through the Red Cross this morning," Manon tells me. "It is from my mother."

"How is she?" I ask as we stroll across the lawn toward some trees. I wonder why Manon has never talked about her father, but then I realize that I never talk about my father. I think I'm ashamed of how he gave up after his accident.

"She is doing all right," Manon tells me, "but Bruges and the surrounding countryside is not. The German navy is nearby, at Zeebrugge, and they take the best of everything. There is not much food. My brother, Florian, has been conscripted by the Germans to work on the docks."

"I'm sorry."

She shrugs. "At least he is still close to home. Many of the young men have been taken to Germany to work."

Manon is trying to be positive, but I see her face crease with worry.

"It'll be all right," I say. "The war can't go on forever."

"I know." There's a choke in her voice and I can see she's close to tears. I put my arm around her shoulders and she leans against me. "Florian is not so strong. He is younger than me and will not do well if he has to labor building docks. And if something were to happen to him, my mother would be alone."

"Your father's not at home?" I ask.

In the long silence that follows, I wonder if I've asked something inappropriate.

"My father's dead," Manon says eventually.

"I'm sorry. I didn't mean . . ." I can't think what to say next, so I just hug her tighter.

Manon sniffs and hugs me back. "You could not know," she says, "he was killed early in the war." She takes a deep breath to get back under control. "Tell me about your family."

"There's not a lot to tell," I say, relieved to be back on a safe topic. "I'm an only child. My dad was a miner until a rockfall crushed his leg."

"That must have been very difficult for him."

"It was," I say. "Mining was all he'd ever known. It was impossible for him to adjust to being helpless and unable to earn money to support his family." I'm being generous to Dad. Deep down I feel resentment and anger. Before I know what I'm doing, I begin to blurt out things to Manon that I have never told anyone else. "I know it's hard for him, but I can't help blaming him for not trying harder. After the accident, the company offered him work as an aboveground ore sorter. He turned it down, saying he wouldn't take a boy's work for a pittance."

"He's a very proud man," Manon says.

"Yes," I agree, "but his pride has cost my mom. He refused to work for a boy's wage, but instead he earns nothing and only sits by the fire with a bottle in his hand, staring into the flames and feeling sorry for himself. You know, when I left to join the army, I said goodbye from the door and he didn't even turn around to acknowledge me. I can live with that, but his misery and selfishness are driving Mom into an early grave. That's why I took the job tunneling—it pays well and I can send money home."

I fall silent, embarrassed by my rant. This isn't how I wanted my conversation with Manon to go.

"I'm sorry," I say at length. "I didn't mean to go on so. I've never talked to anyone about this. I shouldn't have bored you with it."

Manon squeezes my shoulder. "Do not be silly, Alec. It is good to talk, and I am honored that you told me how you truly feel."

We walk in silence for a few steps, then Manon draws away. "This is not right," she says with a smile. "You are supporting me, and yet you are the patient and I am the nurse."

"I'm happy to support you," I say. "I wish I could do more."

Manon turns to face me. She looks serious. "Keep yourself safe," she says.

We are so close that I can feel her warm breath on my cheek. My throat is dry and I am aware of every heartbeat. I'm totally lost in those dark eyes. It would be so easy to lean forward and kiss her. Is this the moment?

"Manon," I begin falteringly.

She smiles encouragement.

"Do you remember when I first woke up?"

She nods and the smile broadens.

"I said—"

"There you are, Manon. I've been looking every-where for you." The doctor is hurrying across the lawn toward us. The moment dissolves. "There's an officer from headquarters here to see you."

"To see me? What about?"

"I don't know, but he said it was important. You should go now. He's waiting by the end of the veranda." The doctor points and we both look over to a smartly dressed officer leaning against one of the veranda supports, smoking and watching us.

"Will you be all right?" Manon asks me.

"I will take the patient back," the doctor says before I have a chance to reply. "Now go."

Manon flashes me a devastating smile. "I'll come and see you later, Alec," she says, "and we can finish our conversation." She turns and hurries across the grass as the officer stamps out his cigarette, removes his cap and steps forward to meet her.

My emotions are in a turmoil as the doctor leads me back to the veranda. I'm frustrated that we were inter-rupted at the perfect moment for me to tell Manon how

I felt about her. I'm annoyed at my dad—if I hadn't been so angry with him, I wouldn't have gone on that rant and I might have had a chance to tell Manon how I felt before the doctor arrived. On the other hand, I'm giddy at the way she smiled at me. Did she guess what I was going to say? Is that what she meant when she said we would finish our conversation later? Does she feel the same way about me as I do about her?

As the sky clouds over and the air chills more, I return to my chair and watch Manon and the officer walk across the lawn, deep in conversation. I'm relieved to see that the visitor doesn't seem to have brought any tragic news, but Manon looks deep in thought at what he is saying. She walks in silence for a long period and then stops, stares at the officer and appears to ask a question. I silently wish for her to look over at me, but she is too preoccupied.

Eventually, the two seem to reach some kind of conclusion. Manon nods—reluctantly, I fancy—and the officer replaces his cap and disappears around the side of the villa. I am eager to hear what news he brought, but Manon is in no hurry to join me. She moves slowly back and forth, staring at the ground. I am about to go to her when she looks up. She stands stock-still and stares at me. Her expression is hard to read, but it is so intense that I freeze at the top of the steps down to the lawn. For an age we stare at each other, then Manon smiles at me. It's not one of her bright smiles that can make my knees go weak, but one filled with such terrible sadness that my heart sinks and I feel like weeping. She waves at me and then, head down, follows the officer round the side of the building.

It takes me a moment to recover, but when I do, I stumble down the steps and stagger as fast as I can across the lawn. There is no sign of Manon or the officer.

I wander the grounds and corridors of the hospital, in hopes of finding her. I imagine her walking round a corner and laughing at my stupid misunderstanding. We embrace and I tell her I love her. But that doesn't happen, and the sense of doom I felt at that final smile solidifies and darkens. Eventually, I am so exhausted by my wanderings that I have to be carried back to bed, where I fall into a fitful, dream-laden sleep.

The next morning, I wake up with a glimmer of hope, but Manon doesn't arrive to give me breakfast. I search out the doctor and ask him where she is.

"She left last evening," he says matter-of-factly.

"Why? Where to?"

The doctor shrugs. "No idea. All very hush-hush and secretive. A staff car drove her and the officer away. She didn't even have time to pack—we're to send her possessions on to the army. That's all I know."

All morning I agonize over what has happened. What did the officer say to cause Manon to leave so suddenly?

Where did she go? Why didn't she say good-bye? There are no answers to any of those questions. At noon, I collect my kit, walk out the front door of the hospital and head back to rejoin the Moles of 169 Tunnelling Company. What else can I do?

CHAPTER 8

Hawthorn Ridge–April-July 1916

"I'm going to have to send you back underground," Captain Philpot says. "Are you up for it?"

"Yes," I reply. I have been on light duty ever since I rejoined the Moles, running surface wires and pipes and occasionally working the ventilation bellows at the tunnel entrance. "I'm fine now and raring to go."

"Splendid. With the big push coming this summer, we really need to extend the Lochnagar, Y Sap and Hawthorn Redoubt mines forward as fast as possible."

"I'm fine," I repeat.

In one sense, I'm telling the truth. Physically, I have recovered from the camouflet explosion, but inside I'm a wreck. I agonize endlessly over why Manon left without saying good-bye, but all that does is take me on an exhausting, futile emotional spiral. I've concluded that she really didn't care about me—and why should she? I'm just a hick kid from some tiny place she's never heard of. I tell myself that I created a complete childish fantasy around her just because she was kind to me. She offered comfort and help simply because she's a very good nurse, and in my turmoil after the explosion, I confused that with falling in love. The officer that last day was probably ordering her to a new assignment, and she hadn't even thought to say good-bye to one patient among many—especially one who rambled on so emotionally about his family.

But then I wake up in the middle of the night with her face floating in the darkness before me, that terrible sadness in her eyes, and I know that I *did* love her—that I *do* love her—and that she loved me as well. She must have. I was never very good at hiding how I felt, and she looked at me in a way she didn't with her other patients. She was always concerned, friendly and smiling, but there was much more than that in her eyes when we had that conversation on the lawn that last day. So why did she leave without saying good-bye?

After I go back underground, I totally immerse myself in my work, volunteering for extra shifts, spending more hours than I have to listening in the darkness, pushing myself to the limit and beyond. It helps that I have little time to dwell on Manon—then in May I discover that Eddie is stationed nearby and go and visit him. It's wonderful to see my friend again and hear about his life as a flyer, although there's a hard edge to his voice when he talks about the young pilots coming out and getting themselves killed before he even learns their names. I suppose everyone out here in this war has some of that hard edge. I know I have since the deaths of Harrington and Bernie. Philpot has been very supportive, but I still feel guilt at my failure to warn Harrington in time. At least Ewan escaped and seems to have completely recovered from the experience.

I also visit Jack and the other Newfoundlanders. They're to be part of the coming attack and are settling in just down the road. Jack's as cheerful as ever and teases me about being back working underground while he's up in the fresh air.

"I tell you, Alec," he says, "this big push is going to be a piece of cake. We're training on ground just like the land in front of Beaumont-Hamel. All we have to do is walk forward. There won't be any Fritz left to fight us. The artillery and you mining boys will have seen to that."

"I'll do my best," I say.

"You do that, but remember—we'll be long gone before you crawl out of your hole. You'll need to run fast to catch us before we get to Berlin."

It's good to joke, talk about home and hear a familiar accent. Jack and the others have an infectious enthusiasm that pushes the worries out of my mind for a few hours. They're thrilled to be a part of the big summer attack that will end the war. Rumor has it that thirteen British divisions from Third and Fourth armies and six divisions of the French Sixth Army are going to attack after the mines and guns have destroyed the German defenses. I envy my mates the role they will play in that. Of course, I will play a role in the victory as well—setting the mines—but it will be a hidden role. Jack and the others will walk across no-man's-land in the summer sunshine, subdue any shell-shocked defenders left and take the war back into open country.

As the big attack nears, we work feverishly to complete the mines that will be blown up at zero hour. The 169th are working on one underneath a German strongpoint, the Hawthorn Redoubt, that dominates the ridge in front of Beaumont-Hamel. The tunnel's a major undertaking, over one thousand feet long and more than eighty feet deep. This is very different from the short defensive tunnels we're used to digging.

Here our primary goal is to make as much headway as possible through the hard chalk. The work is noisy, but there seems to be little or no German countermining in this area.

Through April and May, we make good progress—thirty-five feet in one twenty-four-hour period—and by June we're within one hundred feet of our goal. Things slow down now. We can't afford the noise of fast work, so we must wet the chalk and pry individual pieces off the tunnel face by hand. On June 22, the mine is finally complete, and 40,600 pounds of ammonal explosive is packed into the chamber beneath the unsuspecting Germans. The detonators are placed and tested, and wires run back along the tunnel to the mine entrance, where Captain Philpot will set off the explosion. He has chosen Ewan and me to be his assistants. I'm scared of being in our firing-line trenches at zero hour, but thrilled I will have a grandstand view of our great attack. I am hoping that later that day, I will be able to move south to help the Newfoundlanders celebrate their victory.

This will be one of the biggest explosions in history, and it will certainly blow a huge hole through the German lines. As the big day nears, the excitement becomes an almost physical presence. Light railways, carts, mules, horses and burdened soldiers spend night after night bringing up mountains of shells, weapons,

A STOCKPILE OF SHELL CASES.

ammunition, trenching tools, food—everything that our victorious soldiers will need in support as they advance. Behind the lines, cavalry regiments carry out mock charges, soldiers storm fake trenches, and doctors and nurses prepare casualty clearing stations for the wounded. Above us, swirling shapes fight for dominance of the skies over the battlefield.

On June 24, the artillery preparation begins. At times, it seems as if we exist under a solid dome of flying steel and explosives. We are told to prepare the mine for detonation on June 29. On June 28, we're told there will be a forty-eight-hour delay because of the miserable weather. The tension is almost unbearable, but what must it be like for the surviving Germans huddled beneath this incredible bombardment? Is the war about to end?

At dawn on July 1, hours before the great attack is due to start, Captain Philpot has Ewan and me in place, crammed into the mouth of the Hawthorn tunnel. He's terrified that he'll make the electrical connections to blow the mine and nothing will happen.

"I'll just check the circuits once more," he says shortly after 7:00 a.m. It's thirty minutes before zero hour and everyone is a bundle of sleep-deprived nerves. The trenches around us are packed with soldiers busily fixing bayonets, adjusting equipment and waiting. Occasionally German shells and mortar bombs explode nearby, and I pray that none land directly in the crowded trenches.

Although we are side by side, Captain Philpot, Ewan and I have to shout to make ourselves heard above the dreadful clamor of the guns. The roar of the artillery is continuous, and when we occasionally peer out over no-man's-land, the German trenches are barely visible beneath a swirling cloud of gray smoke. I wonder if Eddie's up above somewhere in his fragile contraption of canvas and string.

"You've checked those circuits five times since we got here," Ewan points out.

Philpot merely grunts and busies himself with the wires. I truly believe he's more afraid of his precious mine not exploding than he is of being killed by a German shell.

"It makes no sense," he says after a few minutes.

"Is there a problem?" I ask, suddenly worried.

"Oh, no. The wiring's fine." He says this as if I'm stupid to be worrying. "I meant setting off the mine at 7:20—ten minutes before zero hour."

"The Royal Fusiliers are supposed to take the crater so that we have a foothold before the attack," Ewan replies. "Besides, didn't the commanding officer say that he didn't want his advancing troops caught by debris from the explosion?"

"Yes, yes, I'm aware of all that," the captain says testily. "But a mine this size is going to be heard all along the front. It's bound to give Fritz warning that the attack's about to come."

"But won't the soldiers in the front line be so stunned by the artillery barrage that they won't know what's happening?" I ask. "I heard that the first wave will walk unopposed across the German front lines."

"I hope you're right," Philpot says. "But remember, the artillery barrage will have to stop at 7:20 for the Fusiliers to attack. By the time the others go forward at 7:30, Fritz will have had ten minutes to get ready. Personally, I'd rather see a few casualties from falling rock than give Fritz the time to set up his machine guns while the Fusiliers are still stumbling over no-man's-land."

We sit in silence for a while, Philpot staring obsessively at his watch, me wondering if he's right about the mine going off too early. Eventually, he breaks the silence.

"Look, Alec, there's still twelve minutes to go. We won't see anything from in here. Why don't you go outside and watch the mine go up. One of us should see the results of our handiwork. If you hurry to the right, you'll have time to get to that spot where the trench bulges out. Ewan and I can manage here, and it should be a spectacular show."

I'm torn between wanting to be in at the moment of detonation and wanting to witness the great event, but I know by now that what Captain Philpot has phrased as a friendly suggestion is actually an order. I climb out of the tunnel entrance and force my way along the crowded trench. The German shelling is heavier than before, and there are several places where the edge of the trench has been blown in and I have to duck low. Do the Germans suspect that zero hour's only a few minutes away?

Some of the soldiers around me look tense and worried, but most are cracking jokes and smoking with their mates. They might be preparing to set off for a

Sunday walk in the park. Several men wounded by the shelling are led past me, one with only shreds of flesh and uniform where his right arm used to be. At a point where I have to duck particularly low, a shell detonates nearby and I am almost knocked down by the blast of hot air from the explosion. As I hurry on, I feel clods of falling earth and stones strike my back.

Eventually, the trench doglegs to the right. Behind a pile of sandbags there's an officer slowly winding the handle of a bulky movie camera. If he thinks this is a good place to record the event, then I doubt I can find better. I crouch nearby and peer over the sandbags. The land slopes away before me to some dead ground along the road to the village of Beaumont-Hamel, then rises to Hawthorn Ridge, which dominates the view. Directly in front of me, piles of white chalk show where our trenches cross the ridge. To my left, similarly disturbed ground shows where the Hawthorn Redoubt is, beneath which our mine waits.

"Come on. Come on," the officer says to himself, glancing anxiously between his watch and the dial that records how much film he has used. "I don't want to run out of film before anything happens." He keeps turning the handle at a steady two revolutions per second.

As I look back toward the German lines, the floor of the trench bucks violently and I have to grab the sandbags around me. A section of the horizon rises in a huge dome. Impossibly slowly, the dome swells and breaks apart. Tongues of flame burst out of the cracks and shoot into the sky. A grinding roar envelops me and blocks out all other sound. The dome rises hundreds of feet in the air, hurling great chunks of tortured earth and bodies in all directions. Then the column collapses back on itself, and dark smoke billows out and obscures the ridge. I hear the officer with the camera gasp, and I realize my jaw is hanging open. I close it and stare in awe at the destruction we have wrought. Already, the Royal Fusiliers have risen from our trenches

THE EXPLOSION AT HAWTHORN RIDGE.

and are scuttling forward—tiny figures disappearing into the smoke.

As the roar of the mine fades, I cock my head to one side and listen. In the distance, I can still hear the deep rumble of the artillery barrage, but around me there's an unearthly silence. The guns have stopped. I can even hear birds singing.

I stand and watch as the smoke slowly disperses. I can hear the pop of rifle fire and the rattle of machine guns from the ridge. The bombing of our trenches has stopped, but columns of black smoke show where shells are exploding in no-man's-land.

The ten minutes from the explosion to the main attack seems like an eternity. The officer is busy changing the film in his camera. I think to myself that the piles of white chalk around the crater left by our mine look like drifts of snow. Eventually, we hear distant whistles. Hundreds of figures, the men of the 16th Battalion, Middlesex Regiment, rise from the white lines of our trenches, form up and move forward in orderly rows.

At first nothing happens and I think the optimists were right—there is no one left alive in the German trenches. Then I notice that some of the figures are falling. Not dramatically—they seem mostly to simply lie down as if tired. The chatter of the machine guns is louder now, and more figures are lying down. The others keep going at a steady pace, but now German shells are exploding among them. There are no neat rows anymore, just individuals and clumps of men moving forward.

I gradually become aware of someone standing beside me and turn to see Captain Philpot staring at the panorama across the valley.

"The mine worked," I say. "The column of earth must have gone hundreds of feet into the air before it collapsed."

"Yes," Philpot says without taking his eyes off the attack. "It felt as if the entrance to the tunnel was going to collapse in on us, but I fear it did little good."

We stand and silently watch as the machine guns steadily thin the remaining clumps of men on the hillside. It's difficult to believe that I am seeing men die. I feel as if I'm watching the movie that the officer beside me is making. But there are shapeless, silent piles of khaki uniform all across the fields on Hawthorn Ridge.

Still, some of the advancing figures have vanished over the far side of the ridge. And others are being led by an officer waving a stick toward the dead ground in the valley where the German machine guns can't reach. I count about forty figures.

Eventually, nothing is left moving across the valley. The sound of the machine guns quiets, and the German artillery moves back to pounding our front-line and communication trenches. I look at my watch and am amazed to see that it is almost eight o'clock. I'm not sure what I have just witnessed. How many men got into the German trenches? Did they manage to join the Royal Fusiliers who had earlier disappeared into the smoke around the crater? Why did the officer lead those men into the dead ground?

I turn to ask Philpot what he thinks happened. He's staring across at the empty ridge, ashen-faced.

"Have they taken the crater?" I ask. "Do you think the German trenches are ours?"

Philpot looks at me. His eyes are empty of all emotion.

"No," he says quietly. "Dead men can't capture trenches." He turns and walks down the trench, leaving me to stare with mounting horror at the empty fields.

That afternoon, my head full of conflicting rumors of dramatic victory and tragic defeat, I head down to visit the Newfoundland boys. After what happened on Hawthorn Ridge, I need cheering up and am eager to hear how they have done. Perhaps I'll even manage to link up with Jack.

I ask everyone I meet, but I can find no word of what has happened to them. Eventually, I spot a filthy soldier wearing the blue puttees of my old regiment.

"Ain't mor'n a couple dozen of the boys left," he says

miserably when I approach him with my questions. At first I think he's shell-shocked and not right in the head, but he goes on. "We went over at 9:15 to support the first wave." He talks in a flat, emotionless voice, staring into the distance over my shoulder. Then he laughs harshly. "They didn't need no support, though."

"What do you mean?" I ask.

"Weren't no one left alive to support. We couldn't even reach our own firing line, the support trenches was so full of their dead and wounded. We went on all the same, over the open ground. No friendly artillery barrage to support us. No one else attacking. Just us out there against the whole of Fritz's army. Worst bit, I reckon, was going through our own wire." The man swivels his eyes to stare through me. "We had to bunch up, see, and Fritz knew where the gaps were. He had his machine guns nicely trained. Had to climb over the bodies of my mates just to get through."

The man smiles, but there's no humor in it. "Funny thing—those what got through the wire kept going. All bent forward like, as if they was headed home to an outpost 'gainst a strong wind. 'Cept it weren't no strong wind. It were bullets." The soldier gazes off into the distance again.

"How did you survive?" I ask.

"In a shell hole," he says. "Fritz were getting out of his trench and kneeling to get a better shot at our boys.

I dropped into a hole and shot back. Reckon I got a couple. Sure made the rest scuttle back quick like. Then I come back, crawling, running from shell hole to shell hole. Don't know how I ain't dead."

"How many made it back?"

He shrugs. "Couple of dozen, maybe. Course there's probably a few more still hiding in holes out there, waiting for dark. But I doubt there's more'n a hundred that ain't dead or with bits shot off them."

The man falls silent once more and I stumble off in shock. Only a hundred left from the eight hundred who started the attack? Surely it isn't possible. And yet I know it is. Philpot and I saw what machine guns can do to men in the open on Hawthorn Ridge. And Jack—is he one of the fortunate few who made it back? I feel lucky. If meeting Eddie hadn't made me think of flying, I would never have applied for a transfer, and never been selected as a tunneler. I'd have stayed with my Newfoundland mates and, in all likelihood, ended up an inert pile of khaki in the open field between the lines.

I think of all the cheerful boys I met in the regiment— boys eager for adventure and the chance to escape the fishing boats or the mines and the narrow world of the outports. Boys whose families will now receive a telegram or read a name in a long column in the local paper. Boys who will never go home. I feel unutterably lonely and miserable. Why do I deserve to survive?

CHAPTER 9

The Plan—April 1917

"Nothing remotely like this has ever been attempted before." Captain Philpot, Ewan and I are standing in a reserve trench, peering out over a shattered landscape of stripped tree trunks, ruined buildings and barbed wire. Philpot is talking but I'm barely listening.

A plane drones across the gray sky above us. Every time I've seen a plane in the ten months since that terrible day on the Somme, I've wondered if Eddie's in it, but I haven't been able to find him again. I have run into the Newfoundlanders, but I didn't recognize any of them. They were all new boys, replacing the friends I knew. Jack is listed as missing, which means he's been blown to pieces, buried by a shell or possibly taken prisoner.

I've lost my friends and I miss home. The letters from Mom are always cheerful and she's grateful for the extra money I can send, but reading between the lines, I understand that Dad's no better than before and life is just as hard. Sometimes I wish I could go back and help out, but what would I do to earn a living—go on the fishing boats or back down a mine? After all I've seen and done in a year and a half of war, I doubt an outport could ever be big enough to hold me again.

I also think a lot about Manon. I try to push her out of my mind, and when I'm scared mindless or so exhausted I can't think, I succeed. The rest of the time, she's there with that devastating smile, ready to turn my knees to Jell-O and bring a lump the size of Newfoundland to my throat. How can such beauty exist in the same world as the horrors of this war? I hope she's safe.

Our mine on Hawthorn Ridge didn't open the way to the end of the war. The Germans occupied the crater first, and it was those machine gunners who slaughtered the men of the Middlesex Battalion. The battle dragged on into November as the casualty lists grew to little apparent purpose.

After the Somme, 169 Tunnelling Company moved north to Vimy Ridge. There we worked hard digging tunnels and storerooms to shelter men and supplies before the big Canadian attack last week. We did a good job, and Vimy Ridge is now part of our lines. We dug no more major offensive mines after Hawthorn Ridge, but that hasn't deterred Ormsby-Smith. He has a new plan, and that is why the three of us are in this trench near Arras.

Philpot gestures across no-man's-land to where the ground rises gently to a long ridge. "Fritz is sitting on top of Messines Ridge, happily watching everything we do down here," he says. "The intention is to blow him off the top of that hill."

"That'll take a mighty big mine," says Ewan, scanning the length of the ridge.

"Actually, more than twenty mines."

We both stare hard at Philpot.

"All exploded simultaneously beneath every German strongpoint on the ridge. It'll blow the top off and cause an earthquake that will stun any remaining defenders."

I look back at the ridge. It's pockmarked with countless shell holes after years of fighting, but there are several much larger craters.

"Looks as if there's been mining here before," I say.

"Indeed there has," Philpot confirms. "Fritz started it here and blew some big ones under our trenches, but we're catching up."

"If Fritz is so active here," Ewan asks, "how can we hope to drive twenty mines without being discovered?"

"Two reasons. First, several mines are already completed with explosives in place, so we won't have to dig twenty mines at one time. Second, we're tunneling much deeper than Fritz."

"How deep?" I ask.

"A hundred feet or more."

Ewan whistles. "We were only down half that far on the Somme."

"Geology's different here," Philpot explains. "There's a sandy layer at the top. It's okay for mining, but it goes down only twenty or thirty feet. That's the layer where Fritz has been working. Below it there's thirty or forty feet of running sand. Hideous stuff. It's waterlogged sand the consistency of thick soup. Impossible to mine through, and if you break into it, it flows into your tunnel like a river of quicksand. But below the running sand, it's clay—easy and quiet to work in."

"And Fritz isn't tunneling in the clay?" Ewan asks.

Philpot shakes his head. "He uses wooden or concrete shoring, so it's almost impossible to put a shaft through the running sand. We use steel liners, so we can drive a deep vertical shaft through the running sand and into the clay below. Of course, we keep working in the upper level as well, but that's just a distraction so Fritz won't suspect we have deep tunnels. He assumes that since he can't get through the running sand, it's impossible for us to get through it too.

"I brought you two up here to show you the lay of the land," Philpot goes on, "but also to tell you something. There's going to be some reorganization around our move here. A few of our lads are going to be heading off to other units to make way for some new chaps—experts in digging through clay—but I wanted to be sure I kept you two."

Ewan and I look at each other, wondering what's coming. Whatever it is will be a wrench. The tunneling company has become a tight-knit group, and any change is going to be traumatic.

"Ewan, I want you to take charge of a full tunneling squad."

"But I'm only a sergeant," Ewan says.

"I was getting to that," Philpot says with a smile. "I've recommended that you be promoted to second lieutenant. It will mean taking a course, and that won't happen until after this adventure. So for the moment you'll only have an acting rank."

"Thank you." Ewan looks a bit stunned.

"And since we'll be a sergeant short," says Philpot, turning to me, "I've recommended you for that position. You'll be the listener in Ewan's squad."

"Thank you," I say, although I'm not sure how grateful I am. The responsibility of being in charge of other men scares me, and I like the anonymity of being just another soldier. But I'm glad I'll be in Ewan's squad.

"So," Philpot says, "first chance you get, go to stores and pick up the stripes and pips for your new ranks. And congratulations."

"Thank you," Ewan and I say simultaneously.

"Well, now that we've had a look and I've announced the great news, we should get going. Ormsby-Smith's coming by to welcome us. It's his idea to blow up the entire ridge at one time, so he's taking a special interest in it. He also wants to introduce us to the men who'll teach us how to dig through clay."

I think back to Egypt and the skinny, monocled British officer who picked me for a tunneler. It doesn't surprise me that he would come up with the idea of twenty mines exploding at once.

We make our way back along the reserve trenches to the hamlet of Voormezeele. It's just a few buildings straggling along both sides of a rural road. There's hardly a single structure undamaged by German shelling, but the cellars are safe and that's where the 169th is based.

On the far side of Voormezeele we come upon an extraordinary sight: a huge, highly polished, open-topped silver motor car parked in the shade of a line of plane trees. Its seats are deep red leather, and apart from some mud around the wheels, it gleams so brightly that

I scan the sky nervously to see if any German planes might spot it and drop a couple of bombs on our heads. A bored-looking sergeant is sitting in the driver's seat, and Ormsby-Smith stands with one foot on the running board, his monocle firmly in place and a cigarette hanging nonchalantly from the corner of his mouth.

As we approach, he removes the cigarette and says, "Well, Reggie, how are the Moles doing?"

"Very well, sir. Thank you. Keen to have a shot at your ridge over there." Philpot jerks a thumb over his shoulder toward the German lines.

"Splendid. We'll give Fritz a surprise, eh?"

"Indeed we will," the captain replies. "I hear you have some new men for us."

"I have, I have. Clay-kickers."

Ewan and I are standing stiffly at attention, watching and listening. Ormsby-Smith throws his cigarette away and reaches into the car's back seat to grab an odd-looking shovel. To our amazement, he plops down on the muddy ground with his back to the car's front wheel.

"Imagine I'm at the tunnel face," he says, placing the shovel between his raised knees. "In front of me's the blue clay you get everywhere hereabouts—damnable stuff, too soft to work with a pick and shovel, but tough as old boots nonetheless. This is the answer: a grafting tool."

The implement he holds up has an open-ended metal box where the shovel head should be. Just behind it, a crosspiece juts out on either side of the shaft. Ormsby-Smith places a foot on each side of the crosspiece and thrusts the odd shovel forward into the empty air.

"Digs into the clay, you see. Cuts out a nice neat block that can then be carted away. Beautifully simple." He stands up and brushes the worst of the mud off his trousers. "A good clay-kicking team can make twenty-five feet in an eight-hour shift." He throws the shovel back into the car. "I've sent enough clay-kickers to give you a couple of good men for each of your digging squads. They can teach the other lads. You'll be under Fritz's trenches before you know it."

"Sounds like a wonderful invention," Philpot says, although he sounds uncertain.

"Indeed it is," agrees Ormsby-Smith, throwing open the car door. "Well, must be off. There's a war to be fought, you know. Here"—he hands two bottles to Philpot—"best port there is."

"Thank you," the captain says.

Ormsby-Smith closes the car door. "Like the car, Reggie?"

"It's a beauty," Philpot replies loyally.

"Rolls-Royce, you know. They call it a Silver Ghost. Purrs along like a dream. You should try one, Reggie. You'll never get back on a horse again." Tapping his sergeant on the shoulder, Ormsby-Smith barks, "Back to HQ, Forbes." The car grumbles into life, pulls out onto the road and heads down the line of trees.

We stand and watch it disappear, all a bit dazed by the eccentric Ormsby-Smith.

Then Philpot says in a low voice, "I don't like port and I've never ridden a horse."

Ewan begins to laugh but quickly turns it into a cough.

"Well," Philpot says, turning toward Voormezeele, "I suppose we'd better go and meet these clay-kickers."

CHAPTER 10

New Boys—April 1917

"Wait till we clay-kickers get underground. We'll show Fritz what's what."

Ewan and I are escorting a couple of the new boys up to the line to show them around. They are both fresh from civilian life—where they worked digging sewers beneath the city of Manchester—and have had virtually no military training. Ewan wants to see how they react to the front-line trenches.

The new pair are both short and stocky, but in personality they're as different as chalk and cheese. Ernie is the quiet one. He has a broad, cheerful face and a snub nose. He says very little but is always looking around at what's happening nearby. Stan, on the other hand, has a narrow face, and his nose and chin jut out aggressively. He's full of bluff and boasting, and I'm not sure whether it's arrogance or insecurity. Some of what he says makes me uncomfortable—it's reminiscent of what I said to Eddie on the boat over from Halifax. I'm embarrassed by how naive I was then. I've learned a lot since.

"I were the champion clay-kicker in my team in Manchester." Stan's talking almost constantly as we move along the communication trench. "We used to have competitions to see who could work the fastest. I always won. One time—"

Stan's story is interrupted by a shell exploding nearby. It's a small one and the only danger is that a few clods of earth will fall on us. Stan immediately throws himself onto the duckboards on the bottom of the trench. Ernie begins to do the same, but when he sees that Ewan and I are remaining upright, he stops himself and straightens up.

"That was a close one," Stan says, picking himself up off the ground. The front of his uniform is covered in mud.

"Not really," Ewan corrects him. "But don't worry— it takes a bit of practice to recognize the different shells and how near they are."

"Oh, I weren't worried," Stan says. "But better safe than sorry, eh?"

SOLDIERS IN A COMMUNICATION TRENCH.

Ewan and I exchange a look and continue on our way. I don't mind that Stan was scared—that's natural. What bothers me is that he doesn't admit it. As we progress, he tells us a long story about a cave-in that trapped some miners in a tunnel he was working. To hear him tell it, the men survived only because of his cleverness and courage, but I doubt it. The more I hear Stan talk, the more I think he's all bluster and no substance.

As we work our way along the trench that leads to the tunnel entrance, Ewan explains, "We don't begin our tunnels in the front line. Too dangerous, and there's always the risk that Fritz will send over a raiding party and discover what we're doing. The most important thing at the moment is to keep our deep tunnels secret. If Fritz finds out about them, it could jeopardize the whole coming attack."

"Fritz better not come over when we're on shift, eh, Ernie?"

Ernie ignores Stan and asks Ewan, "If we're trying to convince the enemy that we're only working shallow tunnels, wouldn't it be a good idea to have some shallow tunnel entrances in the front line for him to find?"

"Indeed it would," Ewan says with a grin. "And that's exactly what we do. In fact, I'm going to show you one now, and let you see what the firing line's like. When we're fighting our own confined little war underground, it's easy to forget what the majority of the army's going through up on the surface." He gestures to me to go first. "Alec will lead the way. You two follow and do exactly what he does. The trench parapet's blown in in places and there're snipers about, so when Alec ducks, you duck. Got it?"

Ernie nods and Stan says, "Piece of cake."

The firing trench always amazes me with its apparent lack of organization. There's equipment everywhere—hanging from hooks in the wall and lying on the fire step. Some men are peering out over no-man's-land through trench periscopes or carrying supplies, but others are chatting and smoking on the fire step, and some are huddled into funk holes in the trench wall, trying to catch some sleep. Occasional shells whistle overhead, and rifles crack in the distance. The air is thick with the throat-catching smell of cordite from old explosions, the sour smell of unwashed men and nearby latrines, the nauseating remnants of old gas attacks, and underlying it all, the sweetish smell of death and decomposition. As always, I silently give thanks for the tunnelers' reserve billets and the clean tunnels we work in.

"You boys tunnelers?" a soldier with a periscope asks as we pass.

He recognizes us by the work clothes we wear instead of formal uniforms. But he misses the fact that Ewan is a sub-lieutenant. Ewan ignores the omission and acknowledges that we are indeed miners.

"Well, when are you going to do something about Fritz's mining?" the soldier asks. Without waiting for an answer, he goes on. "Have a look at what one of his mines did yesterday." He offers the periscope, and Stan steps forward and takes it. "Look at that tree off to the left."

Stan takes his time surveying no-man's-land. I know he's trying to give the impression of knowing what he's doing, because unless there's a battle or a raid going on, there's nothing to see in no-man's-land. Eventually he swings round to the left and freezes. Even looking at the side of his face, I can see the blood drain. The periscope begins to shake and he stammers, "Oh, God! Oh, God!" He stumbles backward and the periscope falls. I catch it and raise it back up.

What Stan saw looks at first like rags draped over the stripped branches of a couple of trees about thirty yards in front of the firing line. But it's not rags—it's the remains of two soldiers. Their bodies have been torn into grotesque pieces that hang, limp and bloody, from several branches.

"Pretty sight," the soldier says over my shoulder. "There was three boys in a sap out there yesterday evening, when Fritz's mine went up. It weren't a big one, but it were right below them. Two of the boys you see were blown into those trees. We never found the third."

"Take them down," Stan says, his voice shaking.

The soldier laughs humorlessly. "Be my guest. Just walk over and take them down. I'll make sure that Fritz doesn't shoot you while you're at it." He turns to Ewan. "It would be a better plan if you tunnelers had discovered Fritz's mine before he set it off."

Ernie takes a look through the periscope and says nothing.

Ewan follows suit, steps back and says, "I'm sorry for

those boys, but we can't intercept every German mine. We blow as many as we can."

"To my mind, you're not intercepting enough of them. I've seen your cozy billet back in Voormezeele. Come and spend a few days in the front line, never sure if there's a German miner packing a cave full of explosives beneath your feet, and see if you still think you're blowing as many as you can."

The soldier turns back to his periscope. I can understand his anger, but we're doing the best we can and we have to focus our resources on the deep mines. That inevitably means some shallow German mines will go undetected and some front-line soldiers will die. But the mines that we are working hardest on will save thousands of lives in the coming attack. We can't explain this to the front-line soldiers, though, in case they're captured and give away our plan.

Ewan leads us farther along the trench. He ducks behind a gas curtain, down a dozen steps and into the entrance to one of our shallow tunnels. It's a large dugout lined with timber supports. There's a bench along one wall, and respirator equipment is hanging from nails above it. In the center of the floor, there's a wide black hole with a pulley above it. Beside the hole, a miner is working a cumbersome bellows-like contraption to feed fresh air to the tunnelers below.

"Everything going okay?" Ewan asks.

"Fine, sir," the man replies without pausing in his work.

"Fritz set off a mine north of here yesterday?"

"Yes, sir. Only a small one. It didn't damage any of our tunnels."

"No one heard them digging?" Ewan asks.

"No, sir," the man says. "Fritz has so many tunnels around here there're always noises. We only have enough men to follow up the ones that sound close enough to be a threat to our tunnels. Everyone else is working on the deep tunnels."

"I know," Ewan says. "Thank you."

He leads us back outside. Stan is very quiet and stumbles a lot as we make our way back to the communication trench. I have to continually tell him to keep his head down.

On the way back we have to step aside to let through a carrying party bringing food to the front line.

"Watch yourselves at the cross trench about a hundred yards back," the lead sergeant says as he passes. "There's a sniper working hereabouts. Got one of our boys yesterday."

"Thanks for the tip," Ewan says.

We've gone barely twenty yards when there's a crack and Stan's helmet flies off. He screams and collapses to his knees.

I crouch over him, expecting the worst. He's sobbing

uncontrollably and saying, "I don't want to die," over and over again. I examine his head but can find only a long scratch above his ear on one side.

"He's okay," I tell Ewan. "Only a scratch, as far as I can tell. He's lucky."

"Okay," Ewan says. "Help him up and let's get back to Voormezeele. And keep your heads down."

CHAPTER 11

Deep Tunnel—May 1917

The scratch on Stan's head and his experience in the firing line don't stop him talking, but I notice that he does everything he can to avoid being sent to work on the shallow tunnels. He seems to have a lot of headaches and stomach trouble. Ernie, on the other hand, fits in well—quietly getting on with whatever task he's assigned, and taking the time to teach our diggers how to clay-kick efficiently.

A week after Stan was shot, the sergeant who had warned us about the sniper comes to visit. "We got the blighter," he says after we've brewed a pot of tea. "Everyone was looking for him over on Fritz's side of the line, but I wasn't so sure." He takes a sip of tea and lights a hand-rolled cigarette. "I made a fake head out of a sandbag stuffed with straw, drew a face and put a helmet on it. It didn't look like much close-up, but I put it on a stick and let the sniper get a glimpse or two at the low spot. He fell for it and put a shot through the dummy's forehead. I had my mate Charlie watching the spot where we reckoned he was, and sure

SOLDIER TRYING TO TEMPT A SNIPER.

enough, he saw movement in a small clump of trees."

The sergeant tops up his mug of tea and helps himself to another teaspoon of sugar. He stirs thoughtfully while we all wait to hear the rest of his tale.

"I was right," he eventually adds. "He *was* on our side of the line. I took Charlie and a couple of other fellows and we stalked him. Charlie knocked him out of his tree as neat as anything. Funny thing was, he wasn't no Fritz. He was a Belgian kid, no more than eighteen or nineteen. He was wounded in the leg and kept telling us how much he wanted Fritz to win the war.

"Well, we didn't know what to do with him. Charlie was all for putting another bullet in him and walking away, but I said we should take him to an officer." The sergeant takes a long swig of tea. "Didn't make no difference, though. I heard they tied him to a post and shot him the next day anyway."

We all sit in silence as the sergeant rolls another cigarette. I think of Manon. I had assumed that all Belgians hated the Germans, who had invaded their country and driven them from their homes. But maybe it's more complicated than that.

"Serves him right—he nearly killed me." Of course it's Stan who breaks the silence. I come close to hitting him then. Maybe the Belgian sniper did deserve to be executed, but not for scaring Stan.

———

As April turns to May, the pressure to complete the tunnel in time for the big explosion increases. We're making good progress, and I have learned what the different noises mean in clay. It is more subtle work than listening for digging in chalk, and every hour the men are stopped for five minutes to allow me to listen in silence.

———

SAPPER LISTENING TO GERMAN MINING ACTIVITY.

One day in early May, I hear sounds I don't quite recognize. The noises are faint, on the very edge of my hearing. I need longer than five minutes, so I order the crew at the face not to resume digging. For twenty minutes I sit completely still, with my eyes clamped shut and the geophone tight against the clay. My legs are cramping and the cold damp from the wet clay is soaking through my clothing, but I don't notice. My entire awareness is concentrated in my ears, as I try to make sense of the soft noises that come and go infuriatingly.

At last I'm sure. The noises are too soft to be from digging in the sand above us and too regular to be from work filtering down from the surface. They must originate in the clay layer. Any of the tunnels we're working on are too far away for me to hear anything other than a major explosion. So the certainty grows in my mind— I'm listening to Germans tunneling in the deep clay.

I report what I've found, and Ewan and Philpot come down to listen. They can't hear much—I have the best hearing in the company and have spent many hours over the past weeks listening.

"What do you make of it?" Philpot asks me.

"It's intermittent, but I think it's a pick working," I say.

"How far away?"

"Hard to be precise without listening from a couple of spots, but I'd say over a hundred feet for certain. It seems to be off to our left and slightly above us."

"Do they know we're here?"

I don't know if Philpot is asking me a question or thinking out loud, but I answer anyway. "I very much doubt it. My guess would be that they've managed to get a shaft through the running sand and are putting out a tunnel to see what they find."

"Well, we'd better make sure they don't find us," the captain says. "Ewan, tell the men at the face to get back to work but keep it quiet."

Ewan nods and heads down the tunnel.

Philpot turns to me. "Alec, I want you to live down here as much as possible. I want you to learn the individual patterns of Fritz's diggers. Keep track of how fast they're moving and in what direction, and report back to me each day. I'll get some tunneling going in the sand above them to try to mask your work."

"I'll follow them," I say. "We can't have much more than a hundred feet to go to place the mine, so if they're dropping a shaft from their front lines, they must have just started tunneling."

"That's what I think too. I'll talk to HQ about sending out a trench raid to destroy their shaft or dropping a couple of high-explosive shells in the neighborhood to see what happens."

"You'd better come and see this." Ewan is back and he looks worried.

Philpot orders the clay carriers up the tunnel to

make room for the three of us at the head. At the face, Stan is lying on his kicking platform, ready to work. Ewan shines his lamp on the clay. There's a steady stream of water running down it. The clay's always damp, but this is different.

"What d'you think?" Philpot asks. As he speaks, a piece of clay falls off the face.

"I think we should get out," Stan says.

As if in response, a section of the wall bulges out and collapses on Stan's legs. He cries out in fear as a thick river of dirty sand and water pours around him. It's not moving fast, but in no time Stan's covered up to his knees.

"Get me out!" he screams in terror.

Squeezing as far forward as possible, Ewan and I grab Stan around the shoulders. It's awkward in the confined space to maneuver him around the kicking platform and the running sand is up to his waist.

Stan is sobbing and thrashing his arms about.

"Keep still!" Ewan orders.

Stan calms himself a bit and we haul. He moves, but the sand is still creeping up his body.

"On the count of three," Ewan shouts to me. "One. Two. Three."

Bracing ourselves against the kicking platform and the wooden tunnel supports, Ewan and I pull. For what seems like an age, we strain. My muscles burn with the effort. I'm almost on the point of giving up when, with a loud sucking sound, Stan pulls free and all three of us fall back into the tunnel.

The running sand is still flowing through the tunnel face and has almost covered the kicking platform.

"There's nothing we can do here," Philpot says. "Let's get out."

We retreat back up the tunnel, Ewan and I half-carrying, half-hauling Stan, who keeps urging us to hurry but does little to help. Philpot stays as close as he can to the rising tide of sand. After a bit, the sand slows and appears to thicken. We're out of danger, but we've lost one hundred feet of hard-won ground and there's no way we can tunnel back through the sand, which is like porridge. Is our mine going to be a failure?

CHAPTER 12

An Old Friend—May 1917

"The theory is that we broke into an ancient river channel," Philpot says. "The top of the clay's not flat. Thousands of years ago a river cut down into the clay, and then the valley was filled with the running sand. We broke through that ancient valley wall into the running sand."

"So what do we do?" I ask. "We can't abandon the tunnel after we've come this far."

"I agree," Philpot says. "I went down this morning to have a look. The flow of sand appears to have stopped. What we'll do is move back a hundred feet or so and start a new tunnel sloping down. That should take us below the river valley, and when we're clear, we'll angle back up so that we end up where we intended."

"It's a lot of extra work," Ewan comments.

"I know," Philpot agrees, "and it couldn't have come at a worse time. We have to work faster and harder, which means more noise—and we know Fritz is down in the clay looking for us. But there's no choice if we are to have this mine ready for the attack in a month's time. We're going to have to rely on your ears a lot, Alec."

"I'll do my best," I say as confidently as I can manage. I think back to the German trick in the tunnel on the Somme. My failure to spot that soon enough led to the deaths of Harrington and Bernie. Now I have responsibility for this entire tunnel, as well as all the men working in it and all the men who might die in the attack if our mine isn't ready. I mustn't let myself miss anything at all.

I don't sleep much that night, and next day, when Ewan's squad goes down to begin the new tunnel, I'm there, with my geophones pressed against the clay.

The first few days listening in the new tunnel are a waste of time. We've moved too far back to hear anything other than the usual background noise. So I go looking for Eddie. He sent me a letter a couple of weeks back saying he was moving to 56 Squadron, and they're stationed not far away. There's been a lot of fighting in the air throughout April and the casualties have been high, so I want to make sure he's all right. I borrow Philpot's motorcycle and drive over to see him on the afternoon of May 7, a gray Monday with some thunderheads building to the east.

What I find is very different from the makeshift camp at the chateau where I visited Eddie a year ago. Well-built huts are arranged in a line, and there is a hangar and workshop for maintaining the long line of planes parked outside. As I bring the bike to a halt and remove my goggles, I see a familiar figure emerging from one of the huts.

"Eddie, boy!" I shout as I run forward.

The figure turns and stares at me without recognition. I stop in confusion. It looks like Eddie, but he's thin and looks much older.

"Eddie, it's me. Alec from Newfoundland."

"Alec!" Eddie's face breaks into a smile. Now I recognize him, but I can't forget the blank stare I saw before. "Come and sit down. We don't go on patrol for a while yet. Still underground?"

"Still underground," I confirm as we walk over to a couple of camp chairs outside one of the huts. "Much safer than being up in the string bags you work in."

"Those days are gone," Eddie says, his expression serious. "This is what we have now." He waves an arm at the line of square-nosed biplanes beside us.

"What are they?" I ask. "I haven't seen this model before."

"S.E.5s. We're the only squadron with them so far, and they're the only machines we've got that are faster than the German Albatros. Stable too, and easy to fly. We don't lose as many new boys to stupid accidents."

While Eddie's talking, he's staring at the closest plane, which has a bright red nose. His voice is a monotone and he sounds as if he's reciting information rather than having a conversation.

"Why is there a gun on top of the upper wing?" I ask. "I thought we'd solved the problem of firing through the propeller."

"We have. The S.E.5 has two machine guns—a Vickers that fires through the propeller, and that Lewis gun on the wing, which can fire forward or tilt back to fire straight up. That way we can sneak up under Fritz and shoot him down before he even knows we're there. Easy kill."

The way Eddie talks makes it sound much more callous than the dogfights he told me about before.

"Are you an ace yet?" I ask, wanting to change the subject.

"Eight," Eddie says casually. "Most of us are aces in this squadron."

He falls silent and I have trouble thinking of anything else to say. My friend's barely recognizable as the happy-go-lucky kid I travelled to Europe with. Have *I* changed that much too?

The silence is becoming awkward and I'm wondering how I can escape back to my tunnel when someone steps out of a small hut a distance away from the others. A young man in a captain's uniform walks over to us. On his way, he pats the red nose of the closest S.E.5. He looks very young to be in charge of a squadron, but his chin is firm and his eyes intense. He looks vaguely familiar.

"Going up in half an hour, Edward," he says in a strong English accent. "Let the others know."

Eddie nods.

The young man scans the sky. "Light's not going to be the best, but maybe we'll be lucky and manage to jump some Fritzes." He continues to stare up for a moment and then turns to go. As he does, he says, to no one in particular, "Sometimes I get so tired of this killing. I'll be glad when it's over."

"Who was that?" I ask. "I felt I knew him."

"You should," Eddie says. "That's our top ace, Albert Ball. Forty-four kills and counting. He's brought down eight Albatroses so far this month alone."

Of course I should have recognized the twenty-year-old hero. His face has been on the front of every newspaper over the past weeks. I watch as he walks around his S.E.5, examining every detail. He looks efficient

ALBERT BALL IN FRONT OF A PLANE.

and confident, but what did his comment as he turned away mean?

"I've got to go now," Eddie says, standing up. "Glad you could come over. Drop by anytime."

"I'll do that," I say, although I doubt I will. This visit has been a strange experience that I don't particularly want to repeat. I walk over to my motorcycle, but before I start it up, I hang around to watch the squadron, led by the machine with the red nose, take off and climb toward the darkening eastern clouds.

Three days later I receive a curt note from Eddie. The evening I visited, the pilots ran into a fight with von Richthofen's Jasta 11 squadron. Albert Ball flew into a thundercloud and disappeared.

CHAPTER 13

Panic–May 1917

Three weeks after my visit to Eddie, a German pilot drops information that Albert Ball died in a crash on May 7 and has been buried with full military honors. The confirmation that the hero and our greatest ace is truly dead sweeps through the army and the newspapers at home, but I have other things on my mind.

We have made excellent progress with our deep tunnel and are busy excavating the chamber at the end and packing it with thousands of pounds of explosives. The big attack is scheduled for just eight days' time. The trouble is that the Germans have also been busy, and I can hear them working frighteningly close to our tunnel. If they suspect what we are doing and blow a countermine or large camouflet, we will never have a chance to redig the tunnel before the attack.

Because of the need for quiet, the final stages of the work are proceeding painfully slowly. I'm spending every waking hour listening underground, and my geophones now seem like an extra limb. After every shift, I shuffle back to our billet, shovel down hot food if there is any around and sleep like the dead for as many hours as Ewan will let me.

"Grab your geophones." Ewan is shaking me violently. It seems as if I have only been asleep for minutes. It's still dark.

"What time is it?" I ask, rolling over and trying to rub the sleep from my eyes. "My shift isn't until daylight."

"It's midnight," Ewan says. "Something's happened."

"What do you mean?" I ask, fumbling to pull on my clothes and gather my equipment. "Has Fritz broken through?"

"No, but we've discovered an old shallow tunnel of ours in the soft stuff above the running sand. Reggie wants to see where it goes. He thinks it might reach close enough to the beginning of Fritz's deep shaft that we could blow it and discourage him from working too close to our charge chamber. We want your magic ears to tell us if that's true."

"How old's this tunnel?" I ask as we head toward the

firing line. In the distance, a bright white flare explodes and hangs leisurely in the sky over no-man's-land.

"Not sure," Ewan says as we duck into a communication trench. "I think it was begun by the French before we arrived here, and then one of our tunneling companies extended it almost to the German lines. In any case, it hasn't been worked for months, so Fritz won't even suspect its existence."

"Why was it abandoned?"

Ewan stops so suddenly that I almost bump into him. "There were several reasons," he replies. "Mostly it's because this was a particularly shallow tunnel, only twenty feet down or so, so there was always the risk of a heavy shell breaking into it from the surface. There was also a lot of German digging very close. It was thought that they were about to blow a camouflet or actually break through into our tunnel."

This news doesn't make me feel very comfortable. "Are the Germans still working their tunnels at that depth?"

"That's one of the things we want you to find out," Ewan says with a smile.

"Who's coming with us?" I ask.

"Ernie and Stan." Ewan must have read my expression of disgust. "Look, I know you don't like Stan—I'm not fond of him myself—but I can't let him sit back in the billet twiddling his thumbs."

"Of course not," I agree. "And you're right—I don't like him. He's arrogant, thoughtless and pompous. But it's more than that." I pause for a moment, wondering how much I should tell Ewan. He nods encouragement, so I decide to go on. "Ever since the cave-in, Stan's been acting strangely. You've seen how hard he tries to avoid going underground. He's claimed every illness there is."

Ewan smiles. "I know. I reckon leprosy's next. But I can't let him get away with it." His expression becomes more serious. "My hope is that the more he goes back underground, the more he'll settle down."

"Maybe," I say, although I'm far from convinced. "But what bothers me most is the way he is when he does go underground. He's nervous and jittery, hearing noises that no one else hears and seeing bulging walls that no one else can see. He keeps looking back toward the tunnel entrance, and he's always the first one out when a shift is over. You know that if something goes wrong underground, we all have to rely on our mates. I don't want to have to rely on Stan."

"You're right," Ewan says. "But for all his faults he's a fine clay-kicker, and we're under immense pressure to finish the deep chamber in time for the attack. We need Stan. Anyway, this jaunt's just exploratory. We're only going in to see what state the tunnel's in and have a listen. I don't expect any trouble in abandoned workings like these, and the more safe trips Stan makes underground, the more confident he'll become."

"I hope so," I say uncertainly as we set off once more.

We meet up with Ernie and Stan at the tunnel entrance. Ewan issues each of us a Webley revolver, just in case. The revolvers are normally issued only to officers, but Reggie has managed to find a few, since using a rifle in a narrow tunnel is awkward.

Ewan leads the way with Stan immediately behind him, then Ernie and me. The tunnel is damp and the wooden supports bulge unpleasantly in places, but we make good progress. There are several areas where sand and mud have slumped onto the tunnel floor, but they're old slumps and don't block our way. Eventually, when by my calculations we're about halfway under no-man's-land, we come to the end of the tunnel. A major collapse completely blocks our way. We stop and I listen, but apart from faint noises from the surface, I can hear no activity.

I think we're all relieved when we turn back, but after about twenty feet, Ewan halts and examines an old side slump. Sand has collapsed between two wooden supports, and Ewan beckons me forward. I squeeze past Ernie and Stan and crouch beside him. The cavity is about two feet deep. By the flickering candlelight, I need a moment to realize what I'm seeing. At the back of the hole, where there should simply be more sand, there are neat wooden boards. The boards are placed horizontally, not the way we shore up our tunnels. What I'm staring at is the back of the wall of a German tunnel.

"What is it?" Stan whispers nervously.

Ewan angrily waves at him to shut up and points to my listening scope. I slowly lean forward and place my scope against the wood, trying not to think that there might be a German soldier inches away on the other side.

Forcing myself to breathe slowly, I block out the noises that I know are not coming from the tunnel through the wood—the distant crump of shells, the pop of a rifle, the scrape of a spade in a nearby trench, the clang of a dropped hammer by a wiring party. I can feel the sweat running over my closed eyelids, but I pay it no mind. I try to visualize the enemy tunnel on the other side of the wall and imagine what noise I would hear if someone was there—the thump of a booted foot on the ground, the metallic rattle of a tool or piece of equipment, the grumble of a bag of rubble being dragged out, the hiss of whispered conversation or command. There's nothing.

Eventually, Ewan taps me on the shoulder and points back down the tunnel. In silence, we retreat a few feet.

"What is it?" Stan repeats. Even in the flickering candlelight, I can see his eyes, wide with fear, and the sheen of sweat on his pale skin.

Ewan ignores Stan and asks me, "Did you hear anything?"

I shake my head. "Nothing in the tunnel."

Ewan is silent for a long time. "Let's take a look," he says eventually.

"What?" gasps Stan.

"Keep your voice down," Ewan orders. "If Alec can't hear anything, then there's nothing there. Ernie, you go back out the tunnel and bring us a crowbar and pick. Stan and I will wait for you while Alec has another listen just to be certain."

Ernie nods and disappears down the tunnel. The three of us move back to the cave-in and I settle in to listen once more. I become so focused that I almost feel there's a part of me on the other side of the wood. I imagine this is what being blind must be like. My sense of hearing is so sensitive that if I were to hear a word or a cough or a soft breath, the person would exist in my head as vividly as if I were staring into his eyes. But I don't hear anything. The neighboring tunnel is silent, still and black as it stretches off in both directions.

Ewan has to shake me hard to bring me back to our tunnel. "Ernie's back," he whispers. "Have you heard anything?"

"Nothing," I reply. "The tunnel's abandoned."

What I don't say is that there's another explanation for the overwhelming silence—it might be that the

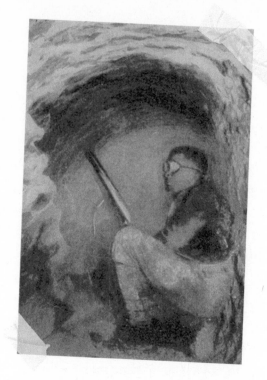

A SAPPER LISTENING FOR ENEMY SAPPERS.

tunnel is very much in use and there is a large explosive charge packed in and ready to blow us sky-high at any moment. No point in mentioning it. Ewan will have thought of that, and if Stan hasn't, I don't want to scare him any more than he already is.

Ewan takes the crowbar, forces it between two of the wooden slats and pries them apart. The crack of the wood splitting sounds like a gunshot in the confined space. I jump and grab hold of my revolver's handle.

Stan whimpers. Ewan stops and we listen—nothing.

"If that didn't wake them up, nothing will," Ewan says under his breath, and attacks the boards with the crowbar. Soon we have a hole big enough to crawl through. Holding his revolver before him, Ewan leads the way. "All clear," he whispers after a minute. "Come on through."

I step aside to let Stan go through. He stares at the hole.

"You go first," I say. I don't want to leave him behind in case he makes some excuse and leaves the tunnel.

He shakes his head.

I put my hand on Stan's shoulder, intending to encourage him forward. His arm muscles feel like knotted ropes under his uniform and he resists even the slightest pressure.

"You have to go through," I say. "It's quite safe. The tunnel's empty."

Stan shakes his head violently. I don't know what to do. Should I continue reasoning with him or try to force him through?

"Hurry up!" Ewan's urgent voice comes from the hole in the tunnel wall.

I'm saved from making a decision by Ernie. In one quick motion, he grabs Stan by his jacket collar, shoves him head first through the hole and helps him on his way with a swift kick. Ernie looks at me with a half smile on his lips, shrugs and follows the others through the hole.

I squeeze through in time to see Stan struggle to his feet and launch himself at Ernie. Before he can make contact, Ewan grabs him and pins him against the far wall. He has his forearm across Stan's neck.

"Are you trying to get us all killed?" he asks.

Stan's eyes are narrow and filled with hate. He's ignoring the arm across his neck and staring at Ernie. Ewan pushes harder into Stan's neck and repeats his question. Stan's gaze flicks over to him. I wonder if he's going to fight back and think how stupid that will be—the four of us fighting in the middle of an enemy tunnel—but the fire fades from Stan's eyes and his body relaxes.

Ewan relaxes his grip. "You can do what you like back at the billet," he says grimly, "but if you ever again put any of my men's lives at risk, I will personally put a bullet in your brain."

Stan looks completely defeated.

"Do you understand?" Ewan asks.

Stan nods.

"What?" Ewan persists.

"I understand," Stan says despondently.

"Good." Ewan draws his revolver. "Now let's see what's going on here."

CHAPTER 14

Enemy Tunnels—May 1917

The German tunnel is larger than ours and much neater. There are duckboards on the floor, and the walls are close-timbered and dry. A ventilation pipe runs along the floor, and several strands of wire are strung from nails near the roof. Using hand signals more than words, Ewan moves to the left, toward the British lines. He leads the way, while Ernie follows behind him making sure Stan keeps up. I take up the rear, continually glancing back over my shoulder into the darkness.

We walk slowly and silently; the loudest sound is Stan's rapid breathing. Our candles cast wildly flickering shadows on the tunnel walls, making it look as if we are being stalked by deformed giants. Every few yards, Ewan signals for us to stop and we listen for the sounds of digging or the distinctive clatter of German hobnailed boots on the wooden floor. After what feels like an eternity, we stop and I hear Stan mumbling, "Oh, God. Oh, God. Oh, God."

"Shut up," Ewan hisses as Ernie and I crowd forward to see what's going on.

In front of us, the tunnel widens into a small room, about six feet wide and the same in height. At the far end of the room sits a pile of wooden crates.

"Looks like Fritz is planning to set off a mine," Ewan whispers.

Stan whimpers. I look up to see that the wires we have been following along the tunnel disappear into one of the wooden crates. I suddenly feel very cold. The mine is wired. If it explodes now, no one will even find pieces of us.

"We have to go," Stan urges, his voice cracking with fear.

"Not yet," Ewan says, handing his candle to Ernie. He steps forward and pries the lid off the crate where the wires end.

"What's he doing?" Stan asks, his voice rising with his level of panic.

"I reckon we must be nearly back under our lines,"

Ernie says calmly. "Wouldn't want this lot to go off under our boys, would we, Stan?"

Stan doesn't say anything, but I get the feeling he wouldn't care if the mine exploded under our trenches, as long as he was a long way away.

Ewan stands up and triumphantly waves two disconnected wires. "That should hold them for the time being," he says. "Now let's get back. We need to blow a camouflet to block this tunnel."

Speed is now more important than quiet, so we hurry along the enemy tunnel. I feel a huge sense of relief after the tension of not knowing what's around the next corner and the horror of maybe having to fight to the death in these dark and confined spaces. In no time we'll be back in our own territory and setting up a camouflet to destroy the enemy tunnel.

We arrive back at the hole into our tunnel and Ernie pushes Stan through. Ewan places a hand on my shoulder to stop me. "I need you to stay here," he says.

"What?" I ask in alarm.

"I need to go back to get the explosives for the camouflet and I need Ernie—someone I can trust—with me. If Fritz runs a test on his electrical wiring, he'll notice that it's not working. He'll send a repair crew along, and they'll discover that we've broken through. They might be able to fire the mine before we're ready to cave in their tunnel."

I stare at Ewan. He's right—someone has to stay here and try to stop a repair party getting to the mine. But why does it have to be me?

As if reading my mind, Ewan says, "I could leave Stan with you."

I shake my head. "I'd run more of a risk being shot by him in a panic than fighting off Fritz."

Ewan smiles.

"Hurry back," I say.

"I will. Good luck." He disappears through the hole and I hear the three of them moving away.

I pinch my candle out so as not to betray my position. I hold my revolver in both hands. The darkness settles around me like a thick blanket. At first I try to peer through it, to make out some shape, but it's absolute. Then I remember my listening training. Ears are what will save my life. I force myself to close my eyes. I know they're useless, but it's hard to cut off a sense I normally rely on so much. I force myself to breathe slowly and evenly. Gradually, the noise of my racing heart slows and quiets. I listen.

It's very different from listening through my geophones. For a start, the air in the tunnel doesn't carry sound nearly as well as the chalk or clay I normally listen through. Also, I have no way of knowing where any sound is coming from. I sit, completely immobile, on the floor of the tunnel. If I move around, I

A WEBLEY REVOLVER.

will become disoriented very quickly. I can feel a ghostly draft of cool air from our tunnel brushing my right cheek.

I try to project myself out into the underground world around me. I try to imagine the world and place the occasional sounds I hear within that frame. A low thump, more felt than heard, is a high-explosive shell bursting a long way off. A sharper sound is a smaller explosion nearby—probably a trench mortar—but whether it's exploding in our trenches or the Germans', I can't tell. A skittering noise at my feet startles me and brings me back to the tunnel, but it's only a curious rat come to check on this intruder into his world.

I have no idea how long I've been listening—but I know I'm half expecting to hear Ewan return—when I get my first clue that a German repair party is on its way. The hobnail boots of the German miners make a distinctive noise on the wooden floors of their tunnels, and that's what I hear first.

I screw up my eyes in concentration. How far off are they, and how many? I can hear two sets of footfalls and pray that's all they've sent down. I open my eyes. There's no sign of light. I hear a faint cough. That's good—it means they're not expecting trouble. They're moving slowly and stopping often, probably to inspect the wiring. Perhaps my rat companion has a habit of chewing through electrical insulation.

I sit in silence, watching and listening while my grip on the handle of my revolver tightens. I have the upper hand—I know Fritz is coming, he is unaware of my presence. Now I don't want Ewan to come back, dragging explosives and detonators noisily along our tunnel. Then I would lose my advantage.

I see the first flicker of light at the same time as I hear a faint, guttural voice. The man must have told a joke, because I hear another voice laughing. Thankfully, I don't hear any other voices. The temptation to empty my revolver down the tunnel and dive back to the safety of my side is almost overwhelming, but I have to be patient. I'm not a very good shot with a heavy revolver, so I have to wait until I can see a good target.

The tunnel slopes down toward me, so the light brightens and I see shadows dance on the walls before I spot the first pair of boots. I aim the revolver as steadily as I can. The legs appear. I can see the second man's boots. The lead man's body is visible now. He's half-turned, talking to his companion. He seems frighteningly close. I can't wait for both men to come fully into view; the lead man will see me before that happens. I fight to keep the revolver steady. The first man is fully visible now. He turns his head back, and I can see his face clearly. He's smiling at what he has just said to his companion. Any second now, he'll see me. I pull the trigger.

Nothing happens.

I've forgotten to cock the weapon. I pull the hammer back. The click sounds thunderous in the confines of the tunnel. The man is looking straight at me now. As he realizes what he's looking at, his smile vanishes. For an instant he looks puzzled, and then his expression slides into terror. I pull the trigger again.

The explosion is deafening. I have a sense of the man falling backward, but I keep cocking the hammer and pulling the trigger. The gun kicks in my hands with every shot. I'm not aiming, simply firing along the tunnel. My head feels as if it's going to burst from the noise.

Eventually, the hammer clicks on an empty chamber. The sudden silence is more disturbing than the overwhelming noise. I peer along the tunnel. An electric torch is lying on the tunnel floor, illuminating the man I was shooting at. He's sitting with his back against the wall, watching me. His right hand is clutching his tunic jacket in the middle of his chest. The material is dark with blood. The man's eyes are wide and his mouth is working convulsively to gulp in air. There's no sign of the second man.

I break open my revolver. The brass cartridge cases clatter onto the wooden floor. I feel strangely calm as I dig in my ammunition pouch for six more bullets. I've loaded three when I hear the panicked voice: *"Hans, bist du in Ordnung?"*

I assume it's the second man calling to his wounded colleague. He's too late—the man I shot has slumped to the side and is either unconscious or dead.

I finish loading my revolver as the man repeats his question a couple of more times. Then a shot echoes down the tunnel. Instinctively, I duck, but the bullet wasn't aimed at me. The torch on the ground shatters and I'm plunged back into darkness. Almost immediately bullets thump into the wooden tunnel supports around me. Wildly, I empty my revolver in the direction of the second man and hurl myself back into our tunnel.

As silence returns, I hear the voice shouting again: *"Lieutenant, komm schnell! Die Engländer haben in den Tunnel gebrochen."*

I don't speak German, but it's obvious that the man in the tunnel is calling for help. I fumble with my ammunition pouch—it's empty. I must have forgotten to close it when I reloaded, and the remaining bullets fell out when I was coming back through the hole. I feel around on the ground but find nothing. I force myself to calm down and listen.

I can hear whispered conversation, but it doesn't sound as if it's coming closer. Then I hear heavy dragging sounds. It takes me a moment to realize that it's the man I shot being dragged away by his comrades. Are they retreating? They must be just as scared as I am, and they have no idea that they face only one man with an empty gun.

I listen as the sounds die away to silence. Then I hear the footsteps and a whispered voice out of the darkness behind me.

"Alec! Alec, are you all right?"

CHAPTER 15

The Mine—May 1917

"I think they've gone," I tell Ewan, finishing off my tale of what happened in the German tunnel. "I heard them dragging off the body of the man I shot." The sudden realization that I have quite possibly killed another human being sweeps over me. "I shot a man," I say, as much to myself as to Ewan and the others. "I looked in his eyes. He'd just finished telling his partner a joke."

"That's one of the hardest things about our job," Ewan says. "We don't see Fritz often, but when we do it's at close quarters. You can't ignore the fact that your enemy is a person when you can smell his sweat and see the fear in his eyes as you shove a knife through his ribs."

I wonder if Ewan's speaking from personal experience.

"He was just a Fritz," Stan says unfeelingly.

In that moment I would have happily exchanged his life for that of the smiling man I shot.

"Okay," Ewan says, interrupting my thoughts. "Let's get this camouflet placed. We'll move along to where our tunnel's blocked. Their tunnel rises, so that will put us lower and allow us to collapse more of their shaft. Alec and Ernie will come with me to help set the charge. Stan, you'll stay here and listen. If you hear them coming back, come and get us. Don't get involved in a fight."

Stan doesn't look happy at the order, but he doesn't argue. I wonder if Ewan has told him to stay just to get him out of our way.

Carrying the explosive charge, detonators, wire and picks, the three of us move along the tunnel as quietly as we can. When we reach the end, we lay the equipment down and Ernie and I begin digging a hole in the tunnel wall. We try to work as quietly as possible, but we have to hurry and I know from experience that the noise we are making will be picked up by any skilled listener fifty or sixty feet away. I hope the Germans have decided to evacuate their tunnel after the firefight.

A SAPPER IN A TUNNEL.

When the hole is deep enough, we pack in the water-proof bags of ammonal explosive. Ewan calculates that it should be enough to cave in a substantial section of the enemy tunnel. Not enough to break through to the surface, but enough to discourage the Germans from trying to cut back through to their mine. Then we'll be able to remove their explosives at leisure and use them in one of our own mines.

Ammonal needs an electric detonator to set it off. Ewan is setting the detonator and attaching the wires when the world goes insane.

The floor of the tunnel heaves and a deep, low roar seems to come up from the ground itself. As the roar increases, pieces of the roof fall like hailstones and lumps fly out of the tunnel walls. One hits my shoulder, knocking me painfully to the ground. Every sense is overwhelmed and I have no idea what's going on. Then a blast of hot air races up the tunnel, knocking Ewan and Ernie over. I feel like my skin's on fire. I'm bruised, deaf, blind and unable to suck enough oxygen into my tortured lungs. I'm dying.

Then, miraculously, everything stops.

I'm not sure whether I'm still alive. The darkness and silence are overwhelming. Then far off along the tunnel, I hear Stan screaming.

"They set off their mine!" Ewan says as he drags himself to his feet. "They must have had a secondary firing circuit that I missed."

He strikes a match and lights a couple of the candles that were blown out by the blast. Ernie's cursing colorfully and trying to stand. His right leg doesn't seem to be working properly.

"You okay?" Ewan asks me.

I nod.

"Good. Go and see what's the matter with Stan, and check out what happened to our tunnel."

I take a candle and head back down the shaft. The air is warm and so thick with dust that the candle doesn't do me much good. I cough harshly as I feel my way along the tunnel wall. I keep tripping over lumps of dirt that have fallen from the roof. Stan's screaming has subsided to a low whine.

"Stan," I say when I'm close, "are you all right?"

"What happened?" His voice sounds muffled and oddly distant.

"Fritz set off his mine," I reply. "Ewan says he must have had a backup firing circuit. Are you injured?" I've reached him now. He's sitting on the floor with his back to me, staring into the hole through to the German tunnel.

"Injured?" Stan asks. "I don't know. My face feels funny."

He must be in shock.

I hold up the candle with one hand and place the other on his shoulder. "Let's go back and see what Ewan has planned to get us out of this."

Stan turns to face me and it's all I can do not to scream. The skin on his face is hideously red and blistered, and flesh hangs from his cheeks and lips in thin strips. His eyes are bloodshot and stare straight ahead, and there is a clear fluid running out of them.

"It's dark," Stan says. "Do you have a candle?"

I lift my flickering candle and hold it in front of his face. His eyes don't react.

"The candles blew out in the blast," I lie. "But it's not a problem. What happened when the mine exploded?"

"I was looking through into the German tunnel," Stan says. "There was a flash and a hot wind."

"We felt it as well," I say. I don't tell Stan that he must have taken the full force of the blast racing down the German tunnel, while we felt only a draft in ours. "You've probably got a bit of a burn. Best not to touch your face until we can get you to a dressing station."

Stan nods.

"Wait here," I say. "I'm going to see how badly damaged our tunnel is. I'll be back in a few minutes."

"Okay," he says in a weak voice.

I feel bad leaving him, but I have to find out if there's any way back to our lines. I doubt it given the size of the explosion, but I have to check. I'm right—within a few yards, our tunnel ceases to exist. It's obvious we will never escape this way, and it will probably take days for rescue to dig its way through to us, if that's even possible.

I return to Stan. "Hold on to my belt," I tell him. "I'll lead the way back."

He takes hold of my belt and we begin our stumbling progress back to Ewan and Ernie. Stan whimpers constantly. I struggle not to think of his face or how we're going to get out of this tunnel.

"Stan's got a burn to his face," I warn as we approach the others. "Have you not found a candle to light yet?"

I stare hard at Ewan, hoping he gets the message. For a long time, he looks past me at Stan, then he nods.

"No luck with the candles yet," he says. "But they wouldn't do us much good anyway, with all this dust in the air. Did you manage to check out our tunnel?"

"It's gone," I say. "There's no way out that direction."

Except for Stan's moaning, silence falls about us as Ewan thinks.

"Okay," he says eventually. "We'll have to go out the other way."

"Toward the German lines?" I say.

"They won't send anyone down for a while, so we'll have the tunnel to ourselves."

"What about getting out?" I don't much like the idea of spending the rest of the war in a prison camp—assuming we're not shot out of hand. I've heard stories of what happens to miners who are captured.

"We'll have to play it by ear," Ewan says. "Whatever happens, it'll be better than dying here."

Stan's whimpering gets louder.

"We could take the camouflet," Ernie suggests. "Fritz's tunnel rises. If we get close enough to the surface, we could blow a hole through and get out into no-man's-land."

"If we're not shallow enough, we risk blocking our only other escape route," Ewan counters.

Ernie shrugs. "Whatever we do is risky."

Ewan comes to a decision. "Okay. We'll take the detonator, wire and as much ammonal as we can carry.

Let's get going before Fritz decides to come down and see what damage his mine did."

"How's your leg?" I ask Ernie. "Can you walk?"

"I'll be okay," he says. "I twisted my knee when I fell. There goes my career playing for City"—he grins broadly—"but I think I can totter along Fritz's tunnel."

We pack up the detonator and wire, and each of us—with the exception of Stan, who seems to be drifting more and more into a daze—lifts a bag of explosives. It's awkward moving down the shaft with all the equipment, the limping Ernie and the wounded Stan, but we make it to the hole through to the German tunnel. We push everything through and follow it into the unknown.

CHAPTER 16

The Shaft–May 1917

Progress along the tunnel is painfully slow. Ewan leads the way and Ernie, in obvious pain, follows. I bring up the rear, encouraging Stan and guiding him as best I can. He appears to have no will of his own and simply staggers along in whatever direction I point him. I think he's gone into shock. But at least he has stopped whimpering—it was beginning to get on my nerves.

The German tunnel is in good condition, but the dust is thicker and breathing is difficult. There doesn't seem to be enough oxygen in the air, and when we breathe deeply we choke on the dust. There's also a sharp smell of explosives. This catches our throats and, hard as we try to keep quiet, forces us to cough spasmodically.

I had hoped that the German tunnel would keep rising, and that Ewan would decide we were close enough to the surface to set our camouflet before we got too close to the German lines. Our plan won't do us much good if we blow a hole and come up in the middle of the German barbed wire. Unfortunately, the tunnel flattens out shortly past the point where I shot the man.

The air has cooled and become more breathable by the time we come to a tunnel running off to our left.

"What is it?" Stan asks as we come to a halt.

"It's a side tunnel," Ewan explains, "running off at about ninety degrees. I think it must run parallel to the German lines."

"It looks very clean and neat," Ernie adds. "I reckon this one's used a lot."

"How do you know? How can you see that?" There's a note of panic entering Stan's voice. "Why can't *I* see?"

We realize too late that we have destroyed the fiction that there is no light.

"Oh, God!" Stan says, his voice rising. "I'm blind!" He raises his hands to his destroyed face.

"Don't," Ewan orders, but he's too late.

Stan screams and barges past us along the main

German tunnel toward their front lines. He's banging off the walls as he runs, but he doesn't seem to care.

"Follow him," Ewan orders me. "We have to stop him before the idiot crashes into a German dugout."

I drop my bag of ammonal, shelter the flame of my candle and set off. Stan's not moving fast and I'm close to catching up when he trips and falls. The tunnel is much wider here and there's a dark room off to the side, but I don't pay any attention to it. Stan is struggling to his feet. He's breathing in loud, ragged gasps and mumbling, "Oh, God!" whenever he catches his breath.

I grab his arm and try to calm him. "It's okay," I say. "We'll get out of here and get you to an aid station."

"I'm blind!" he screams, and swings a wild punch. It connects painfully with my temple and I let go. Stan runs off, but he's become disoriented and heads into the dark room. I hear a few steps and then a scream. I hear some sickening thumps and then silence.

I stand and edge slowly forward into the dark room, holding my candle out as far as I can. The room is cluttered with machinery that appears to be winches and bellows. In the center of the floor, there is a large, round, dark hole. I crouch and hold my candle as far down as I can. The flame flickers in the cool breeze coming from the depths. I can see only a few feet, but I know what I'm looking at: the hole is a deep shaft. It's heavily timbered and a ladder leads down into the gloom.

"Stan?" I say, as loud as I dare. There is only silence. I debate climbing down, but there's no point. Even if Stan is still alive, there's no way I can bring him up on my own. I retreat quickly to the main tunnel and return to report to Ewan.

"This must lead down to Fritz's deep tunnel in the clay." The three of us are standing around the dark hole and Ewan is thinking out loud. "It certainly goes down far enough to get into the running sand, and there'd be no point in stopping before reaching the stable clay. This is the entrance to the tunnel that's been giving us all the trouble."

"Why is it unmanned?" I ask.

"I suspect Fritz brought his tunnelers out before he set off the mine."

"It must be over a hundred feet deep," Ernie says.

We all fall silent. There's no way Stan is still alive after falling that far.

"Should we try to retrieve his body?" Ernie asks.

Ewan shakes his head. "No. But we should go down."

I stare at him. "Why? There's no escape from down there."

"I know," Ewan says. "But we have enough ammonal to seriously damage Fritz's deep tunnel. If we can prevent him working down there, we can finish our mine in peace, and that will make a big difference in the coming attack."

He's right. The attack's only eight days away. If we set off our ammonal in the deep tunnel, the Germans will never get it repaired in time to stop our mine being set, and one large mine might make the difference between success and failure in the big attack. What we do in the next few minutes could save thousands of lives.

Then a terrifying thought strikes me. "We don't have enough wire."

Ewan nods. "I know. We only have a small charge, so we'll have to put it far enough along Fritz's tunnel that it will do maximum damage. We haven't enough wire with us to run from the detonator to a safe spot to fire it from." He looks at me gravely. "Of course I'll fire the charge."

"But that's suicide!" I blurt out.

I don't know what to say. Ewan's prepared to sacrifice himself for the mine we're placing for the attack. Why should he die? I should volunteer. I should, but I can't. I can't bring myself to say the words. And yet I must. "I . . ." I begin, and I stop. I picture my mom getting the telegram informing her of my death. I see Manon's smile. I don't want to die.

While I'm fighting my internal battle, I become aware of Ernie getting down on his knees and holding his candle into the shaft.

"No one has to sacrifice himself," he says, getting back to his feet.

"What do you mean?" I'm clutching at any straw to avoid having to make a decision.

"Ten feet down that shaft, there's water seeping in. That means—"

"The running sand," Ewan interrupts. "We don't need to go down to the bottom to blow in the tunnel. We simply need to place a charge where it will cave in the shaft wall and make a big hole into the running sand. The sand will do the rest."

Memories of the porridge-like substance that almost trapped Stan fill my mind. If we can breach the shaft wall, the wet sand will flood down into the deep tunnel. It'll take weeks to clear it all out, and our mine will be complete and fired long before that.

"Right, let's get going." Ewan is businesslike. "We don't know when Fritz will decide the tunnel's safe to come back to. Ernie, you run the wires back to the cross tunnel and get the detonator ready. Alec and I will get the ammonal down the steps and pack it in as best we can. We should be able to use the steps to hold it in place. Twenty feet down should be enough."

Suddenly we're busy. Ernie limps off with the coil of wire, while Ewan and I fix our candles onto the wooden frame of the shaft and begin manhandling the heavy bags of explosives down the ladder. It's awkward work in the confined space, made worse by the water seeping out of the walls and running over the steps. We climb down as far as the faint light from above will allow and light another candle. Just below us, there's an indent in the shaft wall.

"Are we far enough down?" I ask.

"I should think so," Ewan replies. "There's enough water coming through, and this hollow is the perfect place to pack the ammonal."

We pack the explosives in as tightly as we can, thankful that the bags are waterproof. Ammonal is stable and safe to work with until a detonator is added, but it absorbs water readily and quickly becomes useless.

By the time we have finished and returned to the top of the shaft, Ernie is there with the detonator. He has a coil of wire over his arm and has stretched the rest of it back along the tunnel.

"I'll just nip down and embed the detonator, and then we're done," Ewan says.

Ewan's on the second step when we hear the voice. For a horrifying instant, I think it's Stan, miraculously alive at the bottom of the shaft, but the voice is speaking German.

"*Hallo? Wo sind denn alle? Es ist ein toter Engländer hier unten.*"

Ewan curses. "Fritz must have left the miners down at the deep level. They're asking where everyone is and saying they've found a dead Englishman." He turns and shouts down the shaft, "*Ja, ich komme nach unten.*" He looks back up at us. "I've told them I'm coming down. Even if that doesn't hold them, I should be able to insert the detonator before they climb up to it. Ernie, you go back to the firing box. Alec, you stay here. If I can't make it back up, I'll yell, 'Blow!' You pass that on to Ernie. It will mean the detonator's set, so you"—he looks hard at Ernie—"press the plunger and set off the charge."

"But—" I say.

"No buts. I'm giving you both a direct order."

"Yes, sir," Ernie says, and he sets off back along the tunnel.

Ewan gives me a smile and begins to climb down. I crouch at the lip of the shaft and watch him uncoil the wire as he descends. His progress is painfully slow. The Germans at the bottom of the shaft shout up a few more times. Then, faintly, I hear hobnailed boots on the steps. "Hurry," I urge under my breath.

Ewan has reached the charge. He's no more than a vague shape in the dim candlelight, but I know what he's doing. First he has to attach the wires to the detonator, then he has to cut open one of the bags and embed the detonator as deeply as possible into the ammonal—all the while not allowing the explosive to get wet.

There's a clatter and I hear Ewan curse. Something rattles down the shaft. I pray it's not the detonator.

"*Was ist das?*" The German voice sounds much closer.

"I've dropped my knife," Ewan shouts up to me. "Give me yours."

"*Ein Engländer!*" The hobnailed boots stop.

I dig in my pocket for my folding penknife.

"Drop it down. I'll catch it," Ewan instructs.

I lean out so that I can drop the knife cleanly down the shaft. He'll never catch something that's bouncing off the walls. I hold my breath and let go, watching the knife fall end over end. I'm certain Ewan's missed it when all at once his arm shoots out and snags the falling object.

In the enclosed space of the shaft, the first gunshot almost deafens me. I see Ewan huddle in against the steps, and then his candle goes out. Below him there's another light, dim but visible, as if sheltered by a hand. The sound of boots climbing resumes.

A second bullet thuds into the wooden beams above my head. I grab my revolver, with the idea that I can shoot past Ewan at the Germans—but it's empty. I didn't reload after the firefight in the tunnel and I don't have any bullets in my pouch.

"I'm going to drop a grenade," I shout. "*Eine Bombe!*" I add. I don't have a grenade, but the Germans don't know that.

Ewan catches on. "Good idea. *Lassen Sie eine Bombe.*"

The sound of the climbing boots stops. I drop my revolver down the shaft. It bounces a couple of times against the walls. I hear panicked shouts in German, then a cry of pain. My revolver hit someone. There's silence and I imagine the German miners huddling against the walls of the shaft, waiting for the explosion. When it doesn't happen, conversation breaks out again. They realize they've been tricked, and the sound of climbing resumes. I hope I've bought Ewan enough time.

I can see nothing in the blackness of the shaft. There's only the sound of the hobnailed boots climbing higher—and, softer, the sound of Ewan's leather boots ascending.

"Come on. Come on," I say. It's a race. Will Ewan get to the top before the Germans get to the charge and rip out the detonator?

"Blow!" Ewan's voice comes at me out of the darkness.

If I pass on the message to Ernie, the explosion will kill Ewan. How close is he to the top? How close are the Germans to the charge?

"No!" I shout back. "Hurry!"

Ewan curses me, but I ignore him and listen. As long as I can hear the Germans climbing, it means they haven't reached the charge. I can hear Ewan breathing now. He must be close. At that moment, the sound of hobnailed boots stops. Ewan's breathing is right in front of me. I grab where I think his shoulders must be, gathering handfuls of jacket, and haul as hard as I can.

"Blow!" Ewan screams down the tunnel.

We roll back from the shaft as the earth jumps. There's a huge explosion, and a blast of hot air sweeps over me. The familiar acrid smell of explosives catches my throat. I cough and sit up. There's a flickering light coming along the tunnel toward us. Ewan drags himself upright and shakes his head. Ernie is standing over me. "I think Fritz is coming," he says.

CHAPTER 17

Escape—May 1917

E rnie has heard hobnailed footfalls coming along the side tunnel. Our only choice is to keep going toward the German lines. Ewan sends Ernie on ahead, but he insists that he and I check out the shaft before we go. It doesn't take long. With all the dust and smoke, we can't see much, but the loud sucking noise tells us that the running sand is pouring into the shaft and down to the deep tunnel below. There's no sign of the German tunnelers.

"Okay, let's go," Ewan says. We can hear the approaching footsteps quite clearly now, but they're moving cautiously and haven't reached our side tunnel yet. We extinguish our candles and follow Ernie. We catch up to him quite quickly and have a hurried, whispered discussion in the dark.

"They'll stop and check out the deep shaft," Ewan says. "That should give us some time."

"Time to do what?" I ask. "The only place we can go from here is the German front lines. Are you planning on surrendering?"

"Not unless I have to," he replies. "Fritz knows that an attack is coming soon, and that we're preparing mines to be a part of that. He clears his front-line trenches so they'll be almost empty when the mines go up. Most of the troops are in the second line, ready to race forward when the attack comes. That means we might be able to get into no-man's-land undetected."

"I hope so," I say softly as we set off, but I know we have little choice.

Almost as soon as we resume walking, we come to a German dugout. I listen but hear nothing. Ewan risks a candle. The dugout is empty but luxurious. The walls are solid wood and dry, as is the floor. There are four sturdy bunks, complete with bedding. There are pictures tacked to the walls—mostly of family but also a few landscapes—and clean equipment hanging from hooks. There's a table with cutlery, plates and candles, and a desk with a radio. Ewan picks up a book lying beside the radio and thumbs through it.

A GERMAN DUGOUT.

"A codebook," he says, stuffing it in his belt. "This could be valuable."

We continue along the tunnel and come to a steep set of wooden stairs. We extinguish the candle and climb slowly, stopping to listen often. Both Ewan and Ernie have drawn their revolvers.

At the top of the stairs there's a heavy gas curtain. Ewan gingerly pulls it aside and peers out. "It's all clear," he says and we slip outside.

The sky is mostly cloudless and the moon is almost full, painting the landscape an eerie silver. It's odd to be in the open air after hours of struggling through black tunnels underground. It feels wonderful to be able to see. I grin up at the moon's friendly face, but quickly pull myself back to my situation. The three of us are standing in a German front-line trench.

The trench stretches about twenty feet in each direction before disappearing around a dogleg. It's in good condition, with sturdy sandbagged walls and a solid firestep. A mortar shell explodes to our left and a larger shell whines overhead to detonate in the rear. Somewhere from our lines, a machine gun rattles—a reminder that escaping from the German lines is not going to be our only difficulty.

A flare explodes far above us, casting an unnatural white light over everything and throwing our surroundings into harsh relief. Ewan stands on the firestep and peers into no-man's-land.

"I think I can see a gap in their wire," he says when he steps down. "As soon as the flare dies, we'll go over the top and make for it. I'll go first, then you, Alec. We can haul Ernie up."

Seconds later, Ewan scrambles up the sandbags and rolls over the parapet and out of sight. I follow. The ground slopes away from the trench, so I have to crawl back up. Ewan and I are just sticking our heads over the sandbags when there's a shout from our left. A large German soldier has come around the corner and is shouting at Ernie. Ernie's revolver cracks and the soldier vanishes back around the dogleg.

There's more shouting and the barrel of a rifle appears. A bullet flies wildly down the trench. Ernie and Ewan fire at the same time, and the rifle's withdrawn.

"Leave me!" Ernie shouts. "I'll hold them off."

"No," I say instinctively, reaching down to grab Ernie's hand.

He shakes his head. "I'll keep them occupied while you get away, and then I'll surrender. If they think I'm the only one, they won't chase you. Even if you can haul me up before they pluck up the courage to come round the corner, we'll be sitting ducks out in the open, and I can't travel fast with my bum leg. Besides, you have to get that codebook back."

As we debate, a black grenade arcs over the trench wall and explodes deafeningly. It's far enough away that it does no harm, and Ernie fires off a couple of shots to let the Germans round the corner know he's still alive.

"Go," he says. "Now!"

"He's right," Ewan says. "Good luck, Ernie. Come on," he orders, turning to me. "The sooner we get away from here, the sooner Ernie can surrender." He rolls away and crawls toward the wire.

I hesitate a moment longer.

Ernie winks at me. "I hear that Fritz's prison camps are high class. Better than mucking in with you lot. See you after the war."

"Good luck," I say and follow Ewan.

As we crawl through the German wire, I listen for more shots in the trench behind us but hear none. Maybe Ernie has managed to surrender. He'll be interrogated, of course, but I am confident that he won't give our tunnels away. For the rest of the war, however long that may be, he'll be in a German prison camp. I'm certain it won't be much fun, but at least he'll be alive.

I feel horribly exposed as I follow Ewan into the barren, cratered landscape of no-man's-land. We keep low, but it seems terrifyingly bright, and I know there must be German sentries peering in our direction. I pray for darkness and curse the smiling moon. A machine gun rattles nearby and we scramble into a shallow shell hole. When a flare arcs into the sky, I see that we're not alone in our refuge. Lying beside me, his feet in the filthy puddle in the bottom, there's a British soldier. He's been dead for some time, and the skin on his face has a greenish tinge and is sagging off his skull. I look away hurriedly before I can take in too much detail.

"Poor sod," Ewan comments. "He must have been caught in a trench raid. If we don't want to end up like him, we need to keep moving. When the flare dies, the sentries will be blinded for a few seconds and that's our chance to make it to the next hole. Stay away from old mine craters—they're deep and you might never get out."

As the flare fades, Ewan shouts, "Go!" and claws his way over the lip of the shell hole. We move as fast as we can and fall into another hole, a few yards closer to safety. This time there's no flare.

"Okay," Ewan says, "when I give the word, you go right and I'll go left. That should confuse anyone looking out. Go!"

I climb out and rush to the right. Shots ring out from behind. My foot catches in the roots where a tree used to be and I sprawl to the ground.

"Stay down!" Ewan yells.

There's machine-gun fire from the German trenches, but it's wild—more hopeful than aimed. Another flare lights up the countryside. I hug the ground.

"When the flare dies," Ewan shouts.

On cue, I rise and run. This time the machine-gun fire is farther away and there are only a few scattered rifle shots. We tumble breathlessly into another shell hole.

We progress in fits and starts, feeling more secure as we get closer to our own lines and the firing from the German trenches dies down. We're getting up for one final dash to the wire when Ewan grunts and lies back down.

"Are you hit?" I ask, flopping down beside him. A bullet whines overhead. It came from our own trenches.

"It's my shoulder," Ewan says through gritted teeth. "I can't feel my right arm." He gives an ironic laugh. "This close and I get shot by a nervous sentry."

Another bullet whines overhead.

"Hey," I shout as loud as I can. "Don't shoot! We're on your side."

"There're no patrols out tonight," a voice replies. "What's the password?"

"I don't know," I say. "We're miners from 169 Tunnelling Company. Go and tell your officer. He should know a party of four went underground earlier."

"How did you get out of the tunnel?"

"Just go and tell your officer!" I shout in frustration. "And hurry. I've got a wounded man here."

"Don't move," the sentry says.

I try to examine Ewan's wound. The entire right side of his uniform is soaked in blood and his arm flops uselessly when I lift it. "How are you feeling?" I ask.

"It's an odd feeling being shot," Ewan says, his voice sounding tired. "Felt as if I was kicked hard in the shoulder. No pain. Aches a bit now, though."

"I'll get you to an aid post as soon as possible."

The wait seems interminable. I think back over the events of the night. We've managed to halt the deep German tunnel, but Stan's dead. Although I never much liked him, that didn't mean that I wanted him buried beneath tons of running sand in an enemy tunnel. Ernie's either dead or a prisoner—I hope the latter—and now Ewan's bleeding to death beside me. I know that what we did increases the chances the big attack will succeed. By making sure that our deep tunnel will now be completed in time, we've likely saved hundreds of soldiers' lives. The balance sheet proclaims our night's work a success. The trouble is that Ernie and Ewan have become two of my closest friends, and I don't know any of the soldiers who might die in the coming attack. The personal balance sheet is harder to add up. I've lost a lot and might lose more.

As if in agreement, Ewan sighs. "Think I'll go to sleep now," he mumbles.

"No," I say. "You must stay awake."

"It's hard," he says, his voice becoming more distant.

I've made up my mind to drag him to the trench even without the sentry's permission when I hear a voice. "Come in," it says.

Grabbing Ewan under the shoulders, I stand up and haul him through the gap in the wire. We tumble into the trench and I'm relieved to see a pair of medics standing ready with a stretcher. As they tend to Ewan, an officer comes over to me.

"Was it you boys set off that mine earlier?" he asks.

"That was a German mine," I explain. "We tried to stop it but failed. Did it do much damage?"

"Fortunately, Fritz set it short of our line. We had a few casualties from falling rocks, but nothing too serious. I daresay the wounded won't be too upset at missing the big attack. These mines you boys digging going to do the trick?"

"I hope so," I say. Over the officer's shoulder, I see the medics lifting Ewan on the stretcher. "How is he?" I ask.

"Just a flesh wound," one of the medics calls back. "It didn't hit anything vital. It bled a bit, but we stopped that. He should be fine."

"I have to go and make a report on what happened," I say, turning back to the officer.

"It's a strange world you Moles live in," he says as I squeeze past him.

"It certainly is," I agree.

CHAPTER 18

Earthquake—June 7, 1917

It's almost 3 a.m. and the sky's been clear since midnight. The moon is past full, but it's still bright enough to light up the devastated landscape and allow us to see our planes crisscrossing over the German lines. I wonder once more if Eddie's up there. Ewan, freshly back from hospital with his right arm in a sling and most of the feeling returned, is with me and a few others at a nearby supply dump, where we're sitting on boxes waiting for the mines to detonate to signal the beginning of the attack. All around us reserve troops are huddled down, trying to get a last few minutes of rest. Reggie is in the front line, ready to set off our mine.

Ewan and I are in good moods because yesterday a German deserter told a nearby unit that a tunneler had been captured a few nights ago in his trench. Some men had wanted to execute him, but an officer had intervened and the prisoner had been sent to the rear. It had to be Ernie. He had managed to surrender after all.

"Do you think it'll work?" I ask Ewan.

"If they get the timing right," he says. "Of course, it won't make any difference in the long run."

"It won't?" I ask in surprise. My focus has been on the importance of what we're doing for so long that it comes as a shock to hear Ewan say it's not critical to our ultimate victory. "But surely the mines will allow us to break through?"

"Possibly, but then what'll happen? Fritz will counterattack, and we'll bog down on the next ridge and have to do it all again."

"Then we'll dig more mines," I say.

Ewan smiles. "Let's be wildly optimistic and say that we advance five miles in this attack—not that we've ever come close to that in one day in this war. Give ourselves a year to dig another twenty mines—that's five miles a year. That's faster than tunneling all the way to Berlin, I'll grant you—only a hundred years instead of three hundred. There'll be wild celebrations for the end of the war in 2017."

I laugh but Ewan's right, and his calculations are just

as depressing as the ones he made when he turned down Philpot's bet before the Somme attack. Mines might get us through the German front line, but as we've learned the hard way, there's always another line behind that one.

Ewan peers at his watch. "Shouldn't be long now," he says.

We sit in silent tension. Even if our mines don't end the war, they are an extraordinary achievement. In mere seconds, nineteen mines containing almost a million pounds of explosives will detonate beneath the unsuspecting Germans. Behind us we can hear the deep clanking rumble of the tanks moving forward. Above us the planes fly back and forth, their grumbling engines masking the noise of the tanks from the Germans. Even the artillery is silent, waiting. After the mines explode, our troops will rush to occupy the craters while our artillery will open a hurricane bombardment on the German second line to neutralize the enemy artillery and prevent reinforcements being sent forward. It's all immaculately planned.

As the silence stretches out, my mind fills with questions about Manon. As time has passed, I've become more and more convinced that I do love her, but how does she feel about me? Why did she leave so suddenly, without a good-bye? What has happened to her? Where is she now, and will I ever see her again? Meeting

Manon made everything I have gone through worthwhile. Losing her is devastating.

I'm jolted out of my reverie by an incredible sight. The entire horizon is lifting into the air in a chaos of clouds, smoke and debris. Huge tongues of flame are shooting out of the maelstrom. An unearthly roar thunders in our ears and the ground beneath us shudders violently. The noise of hundreds of our guns opening up adds its counterpoint to the insanity. Thousands of men are ceasing to exist on the summit of Messines Ridge. It sounds, feels and looks like the end of the world. Perhaps it is.

Ewan and I are sitting on camp chairs outside our billet in the ruins of Voormezeele, listening to the crump of artillery from the ridge. It's late afternoon and word is that the attack this morning was a stunning success. Our mines destroyed huge sections of the German defenses, killing thousands and leaving the survivors so shocked and stunned that they could not mount a coordinated resistance. Behind a slowly creeping wall of exploding shells, the Australians mostly walked into their first line of objectives. The defenses stiffened as the attack progressed, but the creeping barrage did its job and it looks as if the day's objectives will mostly be reached.

ONE OF THE CRATERS LEFT BY THE MESSINES RIDGE EXPLOSION.

"A good way to end our work here," Ewan muses as we watch the gray smoke stain the sky above the horizon.

"Yes," I agree. "What's next for us?"

He sips tea from his tin mug before answering. "Reggie reckons this is the end—that we'll be split up among regular sapper units and spend the rest of the war digging trenches and building railways."

The news shocks me. "But Messines has been such a success for the Moles. It proves all Ormsby-Smith's ideas."

"True, but the success here is limited. We've taken another ridge, but there'll be no breakthrough into open country, no glorious cavalry charge across empty fields. The big offensive will take place around Ypres next month. Maybe that will break through, but I suspect it will be just another grind costing thousands more lives. And the Moles are not a big part of that attack. I think this is our moment of glory—or as close to glory as there is in this war."

We sit in companionable silence, pondering what will become of the Moles. I find it hard to believe that it's been only eighteen months since I sat drinking tea with Ormsby-Smith in Cairo. Back then, I was a naive kid disappointed that I couldn't be a pilot and taking this work for the money. I laugh quietly at a sudden thought.

"What's so funny?" Ewan asks.

"Two years ago today, I was caught in a rockfall in the copper mine at Coachman's Cove and decided that I'd join the army."

"A lot has happened since then."

I nod. "And I'm still only seventeen—too young to join the army officially."

Ewan smiles. "We're all much older than we were two years ago."

I think of all the friends I've lost—Harrington refusing to abandon Bernie in a collapsed tunnel at the Somme; Jack rotting with the other Newfoundlanders in a field outside Beaumont-Hamel; Ernie on his way to a prison camp in Germany; even Stan, hideously disfigured and stumbling to his death down the shaft. Of course, there's one other person I've lost . . .

"Mail!" A runner, distributing letters and parcels as he goes, drops an envelope on my lap as he passes. I glance at it, assuming it's from Mom, then I see the London postmark. It was mailed months ago and must have got lost somewhere in the system. It's addressed in an elegant hand to "Alec Shorecross, 169 Tunnelling Company, France."

At first I'm confused. I don't know anyone in London. Then a wild hope fills my head and my heart pounds. I rip open the envelope, unfold the letter and stare at the signature at the end of the short note: "Manon." I feel weak and can barely breathe. My hands are shaking so violently I can hardly focus on the writing.

Dearest Alec,

I hope this finds you well. I do not know where you are, but I am assured that the information on the envelope is enough to get this letter to you.

I am dreadfully sorry that I rushed away from the hospital without saying good-bye. The officer who came for me said that we had to leave urgently, and that I couldn't tell anyone where I was heading or what I was going to do. I thought it easiest to simply leave. I had planned to get in touch with you before this, but my life has not been my own.

I have been offered a way that I can help my country and I have to take it. I will be leaving London soon and so cannot give you a return address, much as I would enjoy a letter from you. I think about you often, and about what you said to me when first we met. I also wonder what it was you were about to say to me when the doctor interrupted us. If it was what I think and hope, I feel the same. Please look after yourself. Until we meet once more after this dreadful war.

Love,
Manon

The fourth time I read the letter, Ewan asks, "Good news?"

He has to ask three times before I answer. "Yes. Wonderful."

"That wouldn't be a letter from that attractive Belgian nurse who almost let me starve to death because she spent every minute looking after you, would it?"

"Her name's Manon," I say.

When it becomes obvious that I'm not going to add anything else, Ewan prompts, "Well, what does she say?"

"She says she loves me."

After another prolonged silence, Ewan stands and

stretches. "Since it's clear from the stupid grin on your face that I'm going to get as much conversation from you as I would from a sick puppy, I'm off to find something worthwhile to do."

I barely notice him leave. I turn the envelope over several times, but there's no return address. What is the opportunity that Manon has been offered? Is it dangerous? How will we find each other after the war?

They are all good questions and I can't answer any of them. But I don't care. Somewhere deep inside I'm utterly convinced that Manon and I will meet again. All the guns, gas and mines in the world won't stop us.

Author's Note

While there was no 169 Tunnelling Company, there were many other units that undertook the work and experienced the adventures depicted in *Dark Terror*. Griffin Ormsby-Smith is also fictional, but he is inspired by Major John Norton-Griffiths, who was instrumental in establishing the tunneling companies of the First World War, and who conceived the idea of the nineteen mines used to destroy the enemy defenses on Messines Ridge. Norton-Griffiths actually did drive around France in a gleaming Rolls-Royce.

The explosion of the mine under Hawthorn Ridge and the subsequent attack were filmed by an official army cinematographer named Geoffrey Malins. The footage became part of a famous movie, *The Battle of the*

Somme, which was released in the summer of 1916 and seen by an estimated twenty million people in its first six weeks in the theaters.

Like many of the stories in my books, the account of the sniper who turned out to be a Belgian boy is based on a real incident. History is always more complicated than we think. Harrington's brave death is based on the story of Sapper William Hackett, who refused to abandon a trapped colleague and died with him. Hackett was posthumously awarded the Victoria Cross—the only one given to a tunneler in the First World War.

The work done by the tunneling companies through the chalk of the Somme and the clay beneath Flanders was extraordinary. As Ormsby-Smith explains to Alec at the beginning of *Dark Terror*, the Germans were far ahead of the British in the use of tunnels beneath the trenches in 1915. Even though the mines at La Boiselle and Hawthorn Ridge in 1916 didn't have the desired effect, they were a major step toward the incredible success of the mines beneath Messines Ridge. Nothing like Messines was ever attempted again, although tunneling and mining continued on a local scale until the war once more became one of movement in August 1918.

The war below ground was a strange combination of hard work, boredom and stark terror—all carried out in incredibly confined, horrifying conditions. Several tunnels, particularly those at Vimy Ridge and beneath the town of Arras, still exist, and more are being discovered by First World War archaeologists all the time.

Before the attack at Messines, several mines were abandoned and their location lost. One exploded in a farmer's field in 1955, killing a cow. A second mine, containing twenty-two tons of old and unstable explosives, lies eighty feet beneath the modern farm of La Basse Cour in Belgium. The farmer, Roger Mahieu, claims the mine below him doesn't stop him sleeping nights. "It's been there all that time," he says. "Why should it decide to blow up now?"

There are not many books or movies about the tunnelers of the First World War. One of the best is the movie *Beneath Hill 60* (there is a tie-in book of the same name). It is filled with extraordinary, accurate details of the lives of Australian tunnelers in the weeks before Messines Ridge.

Glossary

Ace—In the Royal Flying Corps, a pilot who has shot down five enemy planes.

Albatros—A German fighter plane.

Albert Ball—A famous British ace who had forty-four victories before he was killed in 1917.

Ammonal—An explosive used by the British in their mines. It was powerful and very effective as long as it stayed dry.

Beaumont-Hamel—A town that was fortified by the Germans and formed part of the front lines that were attacked by the Newfoundland Regiment on July 1, 1916. Beaumont-Hamel was not captured until November 1916.

Bellows—Hand-operated machines used to pump air into mine tunnels.

Camouflet—A small mine that was exploded to destroy enemy tunnels rather than trenches.

Carbide lamp—An early lamp used in mines prior to the development of electric flashlights.

Cheops (also known as Khufu)—The pharaoh (or ruler) of Egypt from roughly 2575 to 2465 BCE. The Great Pyramid at Giza, outside Cairo, was built as his burial tomb.

Clay-kickers—Men who were specially trained in cutting tunnels through clay. Most had experience constructing sewers beneath the English cities of Liverpool, Manchester and London.

Coachman's Cove—An outport on the north coast of Newfoundland.

Constantinople—The former name of Istanbul (Turkey) when it was the capital of the Ottoman Empire. The aim of the British and French attack at Gallipoli was to capture Constantinople and knock Turkey out of the war.

Detonator—A small explosive set off by an electric current and designed to trigger a much larger explosion, such as a mine.

Drift—An almost horizontal tunnel in a mine.

Duckboards—Slatted wooden boards placed along the bottoms of trenches and over swampy ground to allow soldiers to walk without sinking into mud.

Dugout—Living quarters, usually for officers, dug underground and accessible from the front-line trenches.

Festubert—A French town where, in December of 1914, the Germans exploded ten small mines under the Indian soldiers of the British front lines and made considerable advances.

Fire step—A ledge built up on the floor of the trench so that a soldier could stand on it to see over the parapet.

Fritz—A slang term for a German soldier, pilot or tunneler.

Front lines—The trenches closest to the enemy.

Gallipoli—A peninsula at the eastern end of the Mediterranean. The British and French attacked Gallipoli in 1915, hoping they could advance up the peninsula to Constantinople. The attack failed and the troops were withdrawn in December 1915 and January 1916.

Gas curtain—A heavy sheet hung at the entrance to a dugout or tunnel entrance to prevent gas seeping in.

Geophones—Listening tools rather like stethoscopes, used by tunnelers to detect the sounds of enemy mining.

Grafting tool—A specialized shovel used by clay-kickers.

Hard-rock mining—Mining in ancient hard rocks for base metals such as lead, copper and zinc, as opposed to mining in softer rocks for coal.

Howitzer—An artillery piece designed to fire a shell at a high angle so that it drops almost vertically on the enemy.

Jasta—Specialized German fighter squadrons. The most famous was Jasta 11, led by Manfred von Richthofen, the Red Baron.

Kiwis—Nickname for New Zealand soldiers.

La Boiselle—A French village where a large mine was detonated on July 1, 1916. The crater is still there outside the village to this day.

Loos—The site of a major battle between September 25 and October 14, 1915. This was the biggest British offensive of that year, and the first time they used poison gas. The author's wife's great-uncle was killed in this battle on the first day.

Neuve Chapelle—A French town and the site of a battle between March 10 and 13, 1915. The British broke through in this battle but were too slow in bringing up reserves and could not exploit their initial success.

Newfoundland Regiment—A regiment formed from volunteers from Newfoundland. They fought at Gallipoli and suffered horrendous casualties in a futile attack on July 1, 1916. The site of the July 1 attack near Beaumont-Hamel is now the Newfoundland Memorial and the original trenches are preserved.

No-man's-land—The land between opposing front-line trenches. It had to be crossed to attack the enemy.

Outports—Small and usually isolated fishing or mining villages on the coast of Newfoundland.

Parapet—A raised lip, usually of sandbags, built on the edge of a trench facing the enemy.

Puttees—Strips of material wrapped around a soldier's ankles to keep mud out of boots. The puttees of the Newfoundland Regiment were blue, hence the nickname "the Blue Puttees."

Respirator—An apparatus used for breathing in gas- or dust-filled tunnels during mine rescue operations.

Royal Flying Corps—The British air force in the First World War. It became the Royal Air Force in 1918. Canada did not have its own air force until the Royal Flying Corps of Canada was formed in 1917.

Sap—A short trench, usually dug into no-man's-land to connect a listening or sentry post to the front line.

S.E.5—One of the best British fighter planes of the First World War.

Shell-shock—The First World War name for what is today called post-traumatic stress disorder (PTSD). Shell-shock is a soldier's psychological response to the extreme stress of battle.

Stripes and Pips—Signs of rank fixed onto a soldier's uniform. Sergeants had three stripes sewn onto their sleeves. Second lieutenants had a single metal badge, a pip, attached to a shoulder flap on their uniforms.

Terra Nova mine—A large copper mine on the north coast of Newfoundland. It closed down in 1915.

Vickers and Lewis guns—Machine guns used in battle and sometimes fixed to aircraft.

Ypres—A town in Belgium at the center of a bulge in the British lines. It was the scene of heavy fighting throughout the First World War, most famously the Battle of Passchendaele in 1917.

**Read the gripping first book
in the TALES OF WAR trilogy:**

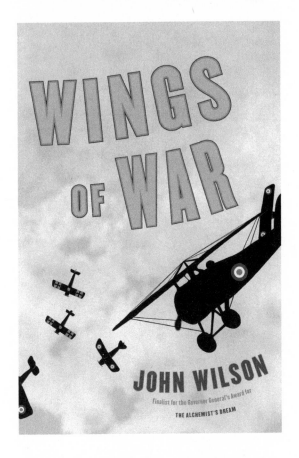

**The daring and dangerous adventures
of a young pilot in World War One.**